A TOUCH OF SUSPICION

Recent Titles by Evelyn Hood from Severn House

DESTINY IN TENERIFE
THE OLIVE GROVE
ROWAN COTTAGE
SECOND BEST

A TOUCH OF SUSPICION

Evelyn Hood

This first world edition published in Great Britain 2001 by
SEVERN HOUSE PUBLISHERS LTD of
9–15 High Street, Sutton, Surrey SM1 1DF.
This first world edition published in the USA 2002 by
SEVERN HOUSE PUBLISHERS INC of
595 Madison Avenue, New York, N.Y. 10022.

British Library Cataloguing in Publication Data
Hood, Evelyn, 1936–
  A touch of suspicion
  1. Suspense fiction
  I. Title
  823.9'14 [F]

ISBN 0-7278-5729-0

Except where actual historical events and characters are being
described for the storyline of this novel, all situations in this
publication are fictitious and any resemblance to living persons
is purely coincidental.

Typeset by Palimpsest Book Production Ltd.,
Polmont, Stirlingshire, Scotland.
Printed and bound in Great Britain by
MPG Books Ltd., Bodmin, Cornwall.

One

K aren shifted uncomfortably in her seat. The meeting had been going on for some time and now the air was thick with smoke from the strong cigars that Forbes Leslie, head of the Sales Department, always insisted on smoking.

Pain began to pulse dully just above one eyebrow; she swallowed hard and looked longingly at the windows, wishing that someone would think of opening them. She should never have come to the meeting, but a dogged determination to put recent events behind her and force her life back into its usual rut had driven her there. Stubborn pride, her housekeeper Anna called it.

As a child Karen had adored the rich formality of the boardroom with its high ceilings and the thick dark carpeting that muffled her footsteps. She loved the polished table with its double row of chairs, and whenever her father took her with him to the offices of Fletcher and Company Limited she had clambered confidently on to the ornate chair at the head of the table – his chair – and scribbled on the pad laid neatly on the table before it, swinging plump little legs clad in short white socks and shiny shoes.

Nobody had ever scolded, for wasn't she the Fletcher heir-ess? Instead, Dan Fletcher had smiled proudly as he watched his dark-haired little daughter bounce on the slippery red covering of the chairman's seat. But now, sitting primly on that same chair, her high-heeled shoes on the thick carpet, Karen felt useless and out of place. There were four other people at the table: Leigh Bailie, the office manager, Edith Carpenter of Personnel, Grant Roberts, in charge of manufacturing, and

Forbes. These people, who deferred to her at every turn because she was the chairwoman, had gained their seats on the board by merit, while her only claim was that she had been born a Fletcher. They were efficient and capable, experts in their different fields of knowledge, while she, head of the textile company that employed them and most of the people in the small town, was quite useless. If she died tomorrow – if she had died at the cottage on the night she had been attacked, she thought queasily – they could continue to run Fletcher and Company smoothly without her.

The subject under discussion at the moment involved some new machinery that Grant wanted to install. Karen, unable to grasp what it was all about, raised her eyes to the two large portraits on the opposite wall, one of her grandfather, founder of the firm, the other of her father just as she remembered him: handsome and arrogant and so sure of himself.

'It's all going to be yours one day, my girl.' She could still hear his voice clearly. 'We're the people that this town depends on. There's nobody like the Fletchers and don't you ever forget it.'

He had raised her to the Fletcher pride, instilling it into her. The only member of the family who didn't seem to have it at all was her Aunt Joyce, and there was good reason for that. Poor Joyce, she thought, then squeezed her eyes tight shut for a moment and opened them wide, a childhood trick she had often used when she needed to force herself to concentrate on what was being said.

'We'd be fools not to try this new thread that Mike Ramsay's come up with,' Grant said just then. 'It's a damned good idea and I think we've got to take the plunge.'

'But can we afford the initial outlay?' Leigh asked crisply, one dark eyebrow raised. 'Do we really want to plunge a lot of money into what, after all, would only be a sideline?'

Grant tossed his pencil on to the table and it landed with a clatter that jarred through Karen. 'It could be more than a sideline,' he said forcefully, glaring at Leigh. 'It could be our future.'

2

'Or our downfall,' Leigh put in.

'You've become very cautious all of a sudden. You're beginning to sound like an old man, Bailie.'

Ignoring the taunt, Leigh opened his mouth to speak and was forestalled by Forbes Leslie, who said, almost apologetically, 'I have to say that I agree with Leigh.'

Grant's hazel eyes darkened, then flicked to the fifth figure at the table. 'Edith?'

'I certainly think the project would be worth pursuing,' the personnel officer said calmly. 'We have to move with the times, and a new thread could be a good investment.'

'Exactly.' Grant ran spread fingers through his fair hair. 'It would have to be a sideline at first, but I can develop it into a very profitable branch of the business, given your support and the extra machinery. One machine would be enough at the beginning.' His eyes were alight. Whenever Grant got an idea he tackled it with tremendous enthusiasm, a boyish enthusiasm that was attractive; and exciting too.

Karen's hands were clasped on the table; glancing down at them now, she saw the broad wedding ring Grant had put on her finger over the diamond engagement ring. Only four years ago, she thought, yet now the rings, and the marriage they symbolised, were no longer part of her life.

'I'd like to consider this carefully before the next meeting,' Leigh was insisting.

'Very well. In the meantime I can arrange a demonstration for you, using one of the existing machines. It won't be as good as the proper machine we need for this purpose, but I can—'

'I propose,' Leigh said firmly, 'that we hold the demonstration until everyone has had a chance to think about it. We can discuss a possible demonstration during our next meeting.'

'But the next meeting won't be for a month – I want decisions now!'

Forbes cleared his throat. 'Actually, Grant, I would appreciate more time to think things over, and the meeting's already gone on long enough.'

'Surely,' Edith interceded, 'the demonstration should go

ahead in the meantime. We need to see this new thread, and any delay . . .'

Her voice seemed to Karen to break up, then fade away as the pulsing developed into an ache centred beneath the broad strip of sticking plaster on Karen's forehead. She put up a hand to massage it, sliding her fingers beneath her new hairstyle's feathery fringe, then dropped her hand back to the table guiltily, feeling as though she had been caught picking at a spot on her face, as she heard Forbes say, '. . . unless, of course, our chairwoman would like to give her opinion?'

'I . . . I have nothing to add.' She never did, but they always deferred to her.

'Then we hold the demonstration back until after the next meeting.' Leigh pushed his chair back from the table. 'I suggest that we close the meeting.'

'I'm afraid we've overtired you, Karen,' Forbes said as the others got to their feet and began to collect their papers. 'I didn't expect to see you here, so soon after coming out of hospital.'

'I was tired of sitting at home.' She smiled at him. 'I'm fine, really.' She glanced at the other end of the room, where Grant was shovelling a thick file into a briefcase.

'Forbes is right.' Leigh put an arm lightly about her shoulders. 'You should be resting, not sitting in stuffy board-rooms. Remember the dinner party Joyce is arranging for tonight . . . you'll need all your strength for that.'

'Oh – I'd forgotten!' Karen couldn't keep the dismay from her voice, and both men laughed. Without glancing their way, Grant walked out of the room. He hadn't got his own way, and Karen knew by the way he moved that he was angry. Leigh followed her gaze. 'He'll get over it; he always does. And sometimes he needs to be reined in a bit.'

'I know.' When Grant wanted something – such as Karen herself, she suddenly remembered with a twinge of sadness for times long gone – he wanted it now; whereas Leigh, calm and steady, took time to think of the pros and cons. Both men were assets to the company and, as her father had realised

4

when selecting his office manager and his works manager, they offset each other perfectly.

'Karen? I was saying, I'll drive you home.' Leigh's voice broke through her thoughts.

'You've got enough to do and the car's outside. I can drive myself home.'

'But—'

'Stop treating her like an invalid.' Edith Carpenter's crisp voice cut into his protest. 'Karen's not made of Dresden china, you know. She'll drive herself home, after we've let our hair down over a cup of coffee in my office. Women only.'

Once in the peace and quiet of Edith's orderly office Karen dropped into a chair. 'Bless you – I was being smothered back there.'

'So I noticed.' Edith poured coffee out. 'I like your new hairstyle.'

Karen put a hand up to stroke the dark hair that until recently had been brushed out to fall below her shoulders, or caught up in a ponytail. She had kept it long to please her father, but recently she had had it cut and shaped into a smooth cap that feathered against the nape of her neck. 'I think I do too, but it takes a bit of getting used to. I get a shock every time I catch sight of myself in a mirror, but I wanted a change . . . and I thought that this fringe would cover the sticking plaster.'

'You're being too self-conscious about it.'

'Am I? Everywhere I go people give me sidelong glances and whisper. I'm being pointed out to strangers as the woman at the centre of a mystery,' Karen said ruefully.

'The plaster will come off soon and the scar will fade, and the gossip will die, as it always does.' As Edith brought the coffee to her, the office assistant tapped on the door then came in to lay a file of papers on the desk.

'Sorry to interrupt, but these need to be signed and sent out as soon as possible.'

'Oh yes. You don't mind, Karen? This will only take a minute.' Edith perched a pair of spectacles on her nose and sat down to scan the papers.

Sipping her coffee, Karen studied the older woman. Trim as always, she was dressed today in a blue-grey-flecked suit that must have been tailored for her. She was beautifully groomed, with good skin and clear eyes, and she had the timeless type of bone structure that made it almost impossible to calculate her age. Her hair, always kept short and with never a strand out of place, was shot through with highlights that made it difficult to tell whether it was light brown or turning to a silvery white. She had been Dan Fletcher's secretary for all the time Karen was growing up, and after his death almost two years earlier she had created the Personnel and Customer Services Department, where she managed everything from hiring and firing to dealing tactfully with difficult clients.

'That's that,' she announced, closing the file and giving it to her assistant, who left the room.

'I wish my father had set me to work in the office when I left school, Edith,' Karen said. 'Then you could have taken me under your wing. Do you realise that I know nothing at all about the business? I sit through these meetings without understanding a word.'

Edith raised an eyebrow. 'You don't have to understand anything – Dan made sure that Forbes and Leigh and Grant and I saw to that side of things. He didn't want you to have to work all your life for the company as he had, and your grandfather before him.'

'There's surely more to life than just being a figurehead.'

'There's a lot of living to do. You're young yet; you have money and friends and a lovely home . . .'

'And a broken marriage.'

For a long moment Edith studied her with cool grey eyes; then she said, 'At least you and Grant hung on to the marriage until after Dan's death, and you both worked hard to hide your problems from him. It would have broken his heart if he had known the truth.'

'We were about to tell him when he . . .' Almost two years later, Karen still couldn't talk about her father's sudden death from a massive heart attack.

'But you didn't, and that's what you have to keep telling yourself,' Edith said. 'Is your head bad?'

Karen hadn't even realised that she was caressing the plaster again. 'This is just a habit, like poking a tongue into a broken tooth,' she began; then, as the older woman gave her a long, steady look, 'It's twingeing a bit.'

'You should have stayed home.'

'And let Joyce cluck over me like a broody hen? I need to get back to normal as soon as possible. Then perhaps I'll remember what happened that night at the cottage.'

'Don't try too hard. If your mind's blanked it all out, then it must have its reasons. The memory might come back, bit by bit, and even if it doesn't, you're only missing a few days. Some people forget everything when they've suffered trauma.'

'It's not just that week between driving to the cottage and then waking up in hospital; it's a whole lot of things that happened before I decided to have a few days in the country.' Karen threw her hands out helplessly. 'I remember some things that happened so clearly, yet other things are fuzzy or blank. It seems to cover a month, at least.'

'But you remember everything that has happened to you after waking in the hospital, so that proves that your mind hasn't been damaged. Why worry about the vague patches now? You went to the cottage on your own and surprised an intruder. He panicked and attacked you. No amount of remembering will turn the clock back.'

'If I could just remember arriving there – finding him there – I might be able to identify him.'

'He's probably a tramp, and long gone by now. You were lucky to escape with just a blank spot, my dear. There was a time when we didn't know whether you were going to regain consciousness or, if you did, whether you might have suffered permanent damage.' Edith shivered suddenly. 'Do me a favour and change the— Saved by the bell,' she added with a grin as the telephone rang. She picked up the receiver, speaking into it in her cool, formal business voice.

'Edith Carpenter. Oh, hello, Joyce.' She raised her brows

at Karen. 'Yes, she's fine; she's right here with me, enjoying a cup of coffee before driving home. Yes, I'll be there; I'm looking forward to it. Bye.'

'I think I heard an anxious hen clucking on the other end of that wire,' Karen said as the receiver was replaced.

'Don't laugh at Joyce, young woman. She's the best aunt a girl could have.'

'I know, and I adore her; but sometimes she drives me mad.'

'She's got her frustrations too,' Edith said. 'When I first came here to work, she was in London, trying to break into acting. It was all she had ever wanted, and it must have taken a lot of strength to overcome your grandparents' disapproval.'

'My father told me that it didn't work out for her and she had to admit failure and come home.'

'It's true that she chose a very difficult profession, but she didn't get much time to find out if it is was going to work. Her mother got into such a state about her that she made herself ill and Dan had to fetch Joyce home to look after her.'

'And then help to raise me when my own mother died. Poor Joyce, she's not had much of a life either.' Karen rose. 'I'd better get back to her. Thanks for the coffee.'

Two

The last thing she wanted, Karen thought as she drove herself home, was to follow in her aunt's footsteps. Joyce had been barely twenty – eight years younger than Karen was now – when she had been brought back home, her hopes of an acting career in tatters, to look after her mother and then her ageing father and her widowed brother's child. She had given her life over to caring for others, and now she seemed contented enough; but Karen wanted more than that, though she was unsure as to just what she did want.

Fletcher and Company employed at least half the adults in the small Warwickshire town of Bradensfield. The factory and the handsome house built by Karen's grandfather when he came to the area after working in the great textile mills in Bradford were at opposite sides of the town, about five miles apart. As Karen guided the car into the side road leading to the house, a ray of sunlight brushed over her left hand, making the diamond engagement ring sparkle. The sudden, fragile burst of light and colour, vanishing as the trees to both sides of the drive cut out the sunlight, was just like her marriage to Grant had been: a wonderful experience in which they had both been swept along by passion and the sheer joy of being together, followed by darkness as their love turned to quarrels and bitterness.

At one time, all she had wanted was to spend the rest of her life with Grant, and she was sure that he had felt the same; but almost as soon as the last crumb of wedding cake had been eaten and the last fleck of confetti swept up, the marriage had begun to crumble. They were too alike, too stubborn and unwilling to compromise. The only thing they were agreed on, by the time the marriage reached its second anniversary, was that Dan should not know the truth. Even though they had stopped loving each other, they both loved her father – the employer who had given Grant his big chance in life – too much to hurt him by separating. It had been hard work, hiding the truth for month after month, and they had been on the verge of telling him when he died in his office. The sense of shock and loss had brought them together for a while, but six months later things were as bad as ever, and they had decided to separate.

She sighed, then pushed the memories away as the car emerged from the drive and on to the sweep of gravel in front of the house where she had lived all her life. As she left the car, a small black poodle rushed round the side of the building towards her, his tail wagging so fast that it went round in circles.

'Hello, dog, did you miss me?' Karen picked him up and hugged him, laughing as his tongue tickled her face.

'Karen, be careful! He's been out in the woods again and you never know what he's been eating,' Joyce Fletcher said from the doorway. 'And you were supposed to be home earlier than this. There's tonight's dinner party, and I promised the doctor that you would have a good long rest first . . .'

'I know, but I wanted to have a chat with Edith. I'm fine, honestly,' Karen said soothingly, wishing that her aunt didn't always have to fuss. 'I still have lots of time to get changed for your party.'

'It's really your party,' Joyce reminded her, leading the way into the large entrance hall. 'Just a small gathering of friends to celebrate your recovery.'

'You think Grant and Belinda will want to celebrate my recovery?' Karen asked, and regretted her words at once when she saw her aunt's shocked look. 'Sorry, I didn't mean that to sound so bitchy.'

'It was rather nasty, darling! After all, you and Grant aren't exactly divorced, and I'm sure you'll be back together one day.'

'I don't think so, Joyce.' There had been too many things said, too many accusations hurled; for the sake of the business, she and Grant had learned to treat each other with civility, but that was as far as it went.

'Though where Belinda's concerned –' a natural blush deepened the colour in her aunt's carefully rouged cheeks '– if you ask me, she's jealous because Leigh's in love with you.'

Karen bit her lip. Before Grant had come along and swept her off her feet she had been engaged to Leigh. She still cared for him, and there was no doubt that the two of them had become closer since her split with Grant; but the scars of that split were still raw and she was afraid of committing herself to marriage again.

'Now, Karen dear,' Joyce was saying, 'I insist on you having a half-hour rest before you get ready for the party.'

Arguing with her was more tiring than anything else, so Karen nodded meekly. 'Half an hour, but that's all,' she conceded. 'Come on, Monty; you can keep me company.'

To her surprise, she fell asleep as soon as she lay down, only waking when Monty jumped on to the bed and licked her face. A glance at the bedside clock showed that exactly half an hour had passed.

'How did you know when to waken me?' She tugged gently at his ears. The little poodle, her wedding present from Grant, was the best and most lasting thing to have come from their impulsive and ill-fated marriage. He had only been six weeks old at the time, and at first her father had been horrified at the thought of having 'a poodle, of all dogs!' in his house; but like everyone else he had become completely captivated within the space of a week by the puppy, who made up for his diminutive size with his courage and charm and infinite capacity for loving. Now Karen could not imagine life without Monty.

After letting him out through the glass door that led from her large bedroom on to a small paved terrace and the garden beyond, she showered then selected a buttercup-yellow shirtwaister from the wardrobe. She was fastening the buttons

11

when she heard a car door slam and her aunt's voice raised in welcome. The first of their guests had arrived.

The thought of the evening ahead suddenly released a clutch of butterflies in her stomach. She swallowed hard, smoothed her skirt with nervous hands, and went out into the hall.

Dan Fletcher, unable to bear the thought of losing his beloved daughter when she and Grant married, had had the upper floor of the house converted into a self-contained flat for the young couple; when the marriage broke down within a year of Dan's death, Karen had moved back to the ground floor, where she now lived with Joyce and Anna the housekeeper. Grant had remained in the upper flat, supposedly until he found somewhere else, and a few months later his sister Belinda, home from Canada after her own marriage ended, had moved in with him.

'What are people going to think, with the two of you living apart yet still under the same roof?' Joyce had fretted at the time.

'It doesn't matter what anyone thinks; it suits us for the moment. Grant's essential to the running of the firm and he has to live in the area. It won't be for long,' Karen had argued. 'Belinda will no doubt find someone else and Grant's sure to find a place of his own soon.'

But Grant was still there and Belinda had found a job in a local estate agent's, and it seemed now that they had settled into the flat on a permanent basis. Not that Karen cared, for the house was large enough to hold all of them. As yet, she and Grant had made no move towards a divorce, although it would happen eventually.

When Karen left her room, the large entrance hall was empty; but as she crossed to the living room, sudden movement on the sweeping staircase made her gasp and shy back nervously.

'Oh, it's only you two.'

'Who else did you expect from upstairs?' Belinda asked, a touch of sarcasm in her voice, while Grant, hurrying down the last few steps, said, 'Sorry if we startled you. You don't mind us coming down this staircase, do you? It seemed senseless to use the side exit then walk round to the front door.'

'Don't be silly, Grant.' His sister, elegant and slender in a bronze-coloured dress that looked wonderful against her creamy skin and sleek blonde hair, came down the final steps. 'Why on earth should Karen object to us using the staircase?'

'Belinda's quite right.' Karen was furious with herself for taking fright. Since her accident everything seemed to startle her. She took a deep, steadying breath and then, realising that Belinda was preparing to lead the way as if she and not Karen owned the place, she added, 'Excuse me . . .' and moved forward smoothly to lead the way into the lounge, sensing a faint twinge of triumph at having managed, for once, to thwart her sister-in-law.

The evening proved to be more of a strain than Karen had expected. It was as though the unknown person who had attacked and almost killed her had managed to turn her into a stranger. Before her accident she and the people who had gathered in her living room to celebrate her recovery had been comfortable with each other, but now the others treated her warily, awkward in their attempts to behave as though nothing had happened. She wished that Charlie, Forbes's wife and her best friend from childhood, had been there to offer the support she needed; but Forbes had come on his own, explaining that Charlie – or Charlotte, as he called her – had had to stay home because one of their children was feeling poorly after having had a tooth out that afternoon.

Sitting on the couch, left to her own devices for a blessed moment, Karen watched Grant's sister Belinda talking to Leigh. Her lovely face, quite sulky in repose, lit up as she laughed and chattered. When Edith turned to say something to Leigh, Belinda immediately moved slightly but in such a way that her back was to the older woman, edging her out. Karen watched, amused and intrigued.

While still in her teens Belinda had fallen madly in love with a Canadian, marrying him within months despite her parents' opposition, and moving to his country. She had only returned, her marriage over, after her parents' death in a sailing accident.

Just like her own marriage, Karen thought. She and Grant had both worked at hiding the truth from her father when cracks began to appear in their perfect union. They had separated within six months of his death.

Since returning to Britain, and to Grant, Belinda's hostility towards Karen had been clear for all to see. She was possessive where Grant was concerned, and tonight she had taken Leigh over completely.

A wave of fatigue swept over Karen and she closed her eyes for a moment, relaxing into the cushions at her back and letting the voices and the background music Joyce had put on flow around her. Then her body jerked upright, the glass in her hand falling to the carpet and her eyes wide.

'Who . . . what . . . ?' she heard herself say as the others turned to stare at her. For a long, frightening moment Karen felt as though she was watching them through thick glass; it was as though they were all inside the room, together, while she was outside, alone in the dark with only a weird sense of danger for company.

'Karen?' She saw Leigh's lips move, heard his voice from somewhere far away, but she was still unable to speak. She saw Grant begin to push his way towards her in slow motion, but Leigh got to her first, reaching out to hold her shoulders. At his touch the glass dissolved and she was back in the room, shaking, perspiration damp on her forehead.

'What's wrong?' Leigh pulled her into his arms, resting her head on his shoulder, stroking her hair. She clung to him, grateful for his strength. 'It's all right, darling, I'm here,' she heard him say. 'I'll not let you go. You're safe.'

'It's been too much for her!' Joyce's voice stabbed into Karen's aching ears; then she heard Edith say, 'She needs air. It's stuffy in here.'

As Edith moved to the nearest window and opened it wide, Grant stood still, his eyes locked on Karen. Belinda, by his side, was also staring, but while her brother's gaze was bewildered, hers was contemptuous.

'There she goes again,' Karen could almost hear her thinking. 'Grabbing the limelight as usual!'

'I'm all right.' She drew away from Leigh, who allowed her to sit up but kept his arm loosely about her. 'I . . . Edith's right; it must have been the heat.' Then she heard herself rush on, 'Who spoke just now?'

They looked at each other, puzzled, and then Edith said slowly, 'I said that you needed air.'

'No, before that. Before I . . . I thought I heard someone . . . something . . .'

'We were all talking,' Grant said.

'Yes, we were. People talk, at parties,' Belinda agreed, her mouth curling.

'But someone . . . one of you, said . . .'

'Said what?' Belinda challenged.

'I . . . I don't know. Just something that sounded familiar.' Looking at the blank faces surrounding her, Karen knew that there was no point in going on. She began to struggle to her feet. 'I think I'll go to bed, if you don't mind.'

'A good idea,' Edith agreed firmly, while Joyce hurried forward.

'I'll take you to your room, darling,' she said, but Edith had already pulled at the old-fashioned bell-pull.

'I think we should leave that to Anna. After all, Joyce, you're the hostess.'

Joyce began to argue, then gave up as Anna arrived, her sharp dark eyes sweeping over the room and settling on Karen.

'I told you that she wasn't up to a party,' she informed Joyce, ignoring the others. 'Look at her, white as a sheet. She's worn out!'

'Nothing that a good sleep won't cure,' Leigh said reassuringly as he helped Karen to her feet.

'Stay, please,' she begged the others as the housekeeper escorted her to the door. 'Don't leave on my account.' Then as

Grant opened the door she hesitated, looking round the room. 'Monty . . .'

'I think he ran out when I opened the French windows,' Edith offered.

'I didn't mean now.' Karen's hand went up to her head. 'Where was Monty when I was attacked at the cottage? Why didn't he try to save me?'

'I expect he had gone off into the woods, the way he usually does.' Belinda's voice was brisk and dismissive. 'And that was just as well, since he's not a guard dog. If he had been there he might have been killed.'

'No, he hadn't run off. We had just come back from a walk and he must have been thirsty, because as soon as I opened the door he rushed into the house ahead . . .'

Karen's voice died away as she saw her own shock mirrored in their faces.

'You remember?' Grant asked sharply. 'It's coming back to you!'

'I . . . I don't know.'

He took a step forward. 'Karen, what—'

'Wait,' Edith ordered. 'The last thing Karen should do is try to remember. She needs rest.'

'She certainly does,' Anna agreed, her hand tightening on her employer's arm. 'And she's going to get it.'

It was comforting to be fussed over by Anna; Karen felt like a child again, safe and protected, as the housekeeper helped her to undress then turned the bedclothes back.

'Seeing you're a bit poorly, you don't need to brush your teeth tonight.'

Tears suddenly filled Karen's eyes and she hugged the woman who had been like a mother to her. 'That's what you used to say whenever I was ill. Don't ever retire, will you? I couldn't bear it if you weren't here!'

Anna untangled herself, as she always did when Karen tried to show her affection. 'Give over; I'll retire when I feel like it. Now, into bed with you and no more nonsense.'

'Where's Monty?' Karen asked as the housekeeper was

leaving. The dog had his own basket in the corner of the room.

'You heard Miss Carpenter say that he went out into the garden when she opened the French windows.' A paved terrace ran along the front and one side of the house, and French windows from the living room, dining room and Karen's bedroom opened directly on to it. 'He'll be back when he's tired, or hungry,' Anna said, and then left.

Karen stared into the darkness, her mind going round in circles as she tried to work out what had happened in the living room. She had been with people she knew and trusted, and yet something – a voice, or perhaps the words it spoke, a movement, or a laugh, whatever it was – had sent a danger signal right through her, and then it had gone before there was time to isolate and recognise it.

She drew the bedclothes up over her shoulders, and buried her head in the pillows, certain that she would not be able to sleep despite the pill Anna had made her take. But against all expectations she soon felt herself relaxing, sinking down into drowsiness, her mind emptying of all thought.

She slept, and then woke to the sudden knowledge that someone else was in the dark room. 'What is it?' she asked sleepily; then, as nobody spoke, 'Is Monty back?'

There was no reply, but at once the choking fear she had experienced in the living room earlier swept back like a thick, muffling fog. As she started to reach for the bedside lamp switch there was swift movement and some of the darkness formed itself into a shape rushing towards the bed. Then something hit the side of her face – something soft, but with a force behind it that pressed her down on to the mattress. One hand was tangled in the duvet, but with the other she tried to push the obstruction away. It stayed, smothering and stifling her.

Three

Panic-stricken, Karen flailed out with her free arm and felt a thin smooth cord beneath her groping fingers. She grasped it tightly and pulled, hearing a muffled crash. Then at last the pressure on her head eased and, as she gulped frantically for air, she sensed swift movement again, this time going away from her.

She kept her eyes shut tightly, even when she sensed that she was alone, and when she heard voices in the hallway, and when the yellow glow of the overhead light fell across her closed lids, not opening them until Anna sat on the edge of the bed, and gathered her up, rocking and soothing her. Because she knew instinctively that her only safety lay in not looking.

If she had looked, she might have discovered that her attacker had a face that she knew well. A face that she trusted.

'I'm perfectly all right and I'd rather be up and about,' Karen argued when Joyce tried to persuade her to stay in bed the following morning.

'All right? You scared the wits out of me,' her aunt fussed. 'I was just going through the hall on my way to my own room when I heard that lamp going over. I got such a fright; I thought you'd tried to get up and then collapsed. And when you said you'd been attacked, I thought . . .'

'Thought what? That this bump on the head had addled my wits? I'm not hallucinating, Joyce; there really was someone in my room last night.'

'How could there have been? The front and back doors were locked.'

'And the French windows? I didn't check mine last night. That must have been how he . . . whatever . . . got out when I raised the alarm.'

Joyce sat on the edge of her bed and took one of Karen's hands, stroking it gently. 'Darling, are you sure you weren't just dreaming?'

'You saw how the lamp had fallen over and spilled that glass of water Anna left on the table.'

'You could have done that in your sleep. And the window was closed when I came in. Anyone rushing out in a panic when he heard me coming wouldn't have stopped to close it behind him.'

'I might have flailed out and knocked the lamp over during a bad dream, but what about the chair cushion lying on the floor? Are you suggesting that I tried to suffocate mys—' Karen stopped suddenly, memories flooding back.

'But why would anyone want to harm you?'

Karen pointed to the plaster on her forehead. 'The person who did this might have wanted to finish the job in case I remembered too much.'

'Now you're being ridiculous! You disturbed a burglar at the cottage and he panicked and hit you. That's over and done with. But this new business . . .' She started to get to her feet. 'I think I should phone the doctor.'

'You will not!'

'Then I'm going to phone Leigh. He'll know what to do.'

'Joyce, I don't want you to phone anyone. I caused enough of a stir last night. Promise me!'

Joyce bit her lip. 'If you say so. But I insist that you stay in bed and rest this morning. Anna will do you a nice breakfast tray . . .'

Karen threw the duvet back. 'I'm not an invalid – not any more. I'm getting up.'

Grant and Anna had taken a liking to each other from their first meeting, so much so that Karen had laughingly accused him of marrying her just so that the housekeeper could spoil him. Even though the marriage was over he had kept up his old

19

habit of dropping in for the chat, so Karen was not surprised to find him sitting at the table with Joyce and Anna when she went into the kitchen. The three of them were deep in a conversation that stopped abruptly at her entrance.

'No prizes for guessing what you three are talking about.'

'I've just heard the latest news and we're all concerned for you.' Grant's voice was level, but his gaze bored into hers as though he was trying to read her very thoughts.

'There's no need to be.' She sat down opposite him. 'Just tea for me, and perhaps a slice of toast.'

Anna tutted disapprovingly. 'Making yourself ill again isn't the answer . . . is it?' she appealed to the others. Joyce regarded her niece with wary blue eyes.

'You need to keep your strength up, dear. I remember my mother always saying, "A healthy mind in a healthy—"' she began.

'I'm not going out of my mind!' Karen snapped.

'Of course not, darling; nobody's suggesting such a thing. But I know from experience that nightmares can be very vivid.'

'If it was a nightmare,' Grant put in.

'Of course it was. What else could it have been?' Joyce asked sharply.

'Karen?'

'Perhaps it was a dream . . . I don't know. It's just that . . .' She shivered, recalling the clear sense of someone else in the darkness by her bed, the chilling menace all around her, the soft, smothering cushion clamped over her face. If she hadn't managed to turn away at the last moment, whoever had come to her room from the darkness would have killed her. 'It was all too real to be a dream,' she said helplessly.

'In that case, I think we should call the police.'

'The police?' Anna's voice shot up the register with surprise. 'D'you want to make fools of us in front of the entire town?'

'If it would put Karen's mind at ease, then I'm prepared to phone them right now.'

'What's the point when I have no proof?' Karen put the

tips of her fingers to her temples. 'If only I could remember what happened at the cottage! It began to come back to me last night, then it just melted away again.'

'Why don't we go somewhere nice today?' Joyce suggested. 'Just the two of us – shopping perhaps, then lunch . . . ?'

'I'd rather stay close to home, if you don't mind. I feel like going for a good long walk with Monty,' Karen said; then, glancing round the room, 'Where is he?'

'I haven't seen him all morning.'

'He wasn't in the kitchen that I remember,' Anna offered.

'When was he last seen?' Grant asked.

'Last night, just before I went to bed.' Karen saw her own mounting unease mirrored in Grant's hazel gaze. 'He must have run out. Didn't he come home last night?' she asked the two women, who shook their heads.

'He'll be out in the woods, or off visiting some little doggie ladyfriend,' Joyce said reassuringly. 'He's done that before – disappeared for hours.'

'He's never stayed out all night before,' Karen said.

'Or missed a meal,' Anna added, the first vestiges of concern for the dog shadowing her features. Joyce looked from one face to another.

'For goodness' sake, don't start working up a drama about Monty now. He'll turn up soon, you'll see.'

'I'll have a quick look round before I go to the factory,' Grant offered, getting to his feet. He opened the back door then stepped back. 'Morning, Helen. You're glowing this morning. New boyfriend?'

The girl who came in three days a week to help Anna with the heavy work giggled as she scampered past him and into the kitchen. She was young and pretty, and Anna kept threatening to get rid of her because she couldn't keep her mind on her work. Now the housekeeper grunted, 'It's a new boyfriend with you every week, isn't it, Helen? Get your apron on and give the living room a good clean out, then we'll see to the bedrooms.'

Reminded, Karen went in to have a look at the room where

she had felt so strange the night before. She sank on to the couch, staring at the area where the others had been gathered, talking and laughing, on the previous evening. Closing her eyes, she tried to will herself back to that moment, but there was nothing – no menace, no chills, and no memory of the voice that had suddenly terrified her.

The phone rang and she jumped and then snatched the receiver from its cradle.

'Karen?'

'Charlie, it's you.'

'I know it's me, but I wasn't too sure about you. Your voice sounded odd there.'

'I was right by the phone when it rang. It gave me a bit of a fright.'

'Lovey, are you all right? Forbes said that you took a bit of a turn last night. I didn't know whether to call or not.'

'I'm glad you did, Charlie. I made an idiot of myself, that's all, but I'm fine now.' Karen took the cordless phone to the French windows as she talked, so that she could look out over the terrace and the lawn, with its flowerbeds, still bright though autumn had arrived, and the thick belt of woodland beyond that kept the house hidden from the road.

'I wish I had been there.'

'So do I. How's Jonny?'

'Recovered enough to go to school today, thank goodness. He was very sorry for himself yesterday . . . with reason, I suppose. It was a difficult tooth to extract, poor little lamb. Do you want me to come over?'

Karen hesitated. As well as designing for Fletcher and Company, Charlie was an artist in her own right, exhibiting regularly and selling well. Karen herself owned several of her paintings. 'What are you working on just now?'

'Finishing off some stuff for an exhibition, but I can easily—'

'No, you can't. You get on with what you have to do and phone me when you're free. We can meet up for lunch then.'

'If you're sure . . .' Charlie's hesitation proved that she was up to her elbows in work.

22

'I'm sure. Speak to you soon.'

When Karen had broken the connection she stayed where she was, hoping to see a small black poodle bounding from the trees and across the lawns, impatient for food and attention; but the only movement came from a bird strutting about the lawn in search of worms.

'Sorry, miss. Mind if I get started in here?' Helen asked from the doorway.

'Of course not. I'll get out of your way.' Karen went past the girl and across the large hall to her own room. Monty was a country dog and it was true that he went off by himself quite frequently.

Karen just wished that he had stayed at home that morning, for she needed the unquestioning love that the little dog had given her since the day Grant had placed him, a tiny bundle of warm black fur, in her two cupped hands.

She went into the bedroom and then stopped, hands flying to her mouth to hold back the scream that bubbled up. Then she flew across the room and wrenched the French window open. 'What do you think you're doing?'

'Checking around here to see if there's any signs of someone going into your room or coming out of it,' Grant said; then his voice sharpened. 'What's happened?'

Her knees were trembling, and she had to cling to the window for support. 'What happened was me coming into my room and suddenly seeing a man standing outside, peering in. You gave me the fright of my life!'

Light dawned. 'Oh . . . sorry, I didn't realise . . .' He reached out a hand to steady her. 'Are you all right?'

'I will be, when my heart stops thundering.' She allowed him to draw her out on to the terrace; it was a soft autumn morning, and the trees edging the wide sweep of lawn were beginning to take on the russet and gold autumn colours that her father had always loved. Karen drew the cool, clean air deep into her lungs and felt her heart slowing towards its usual steady rhythm. 'No sign of Monty?'

'Not so far. I called him at the back of the house, and from the lawn, but he must be too far away to hear. Then I thought that while I was here I might as well take a look at the area round your room.'

'Did you find anything?'

'Nothing. If there was an intruder, he left no trace.'

'Grant, do you think I'm making a fuss about nothing?'

'I know you too well to think that. I believe that you got a bad fright last night, but at the same time, it might have been a vivid dream resulting from whatever happened earlier, when we were all together. What was that all about?'

'I don't know. It was as though I had heard a voice, or a phrase, that frightened me.'

'That doesn't seem possible. There were no strangers in the room, nobody you had cause to fear.'

'I know.' She realised that she was caressing the plaster on her head again, and pulled her hand away from it, summoning up a smile. 'Perhaps I really am going mad. I think Joyce suspects it.'

'She doesn't, and you're not,' he said crisply; then, glancing at his watch, 'I have to go. Let me know if there's anything else, will you? Not that there will be.'

Belinda Solomon was checking her appearance before the mirror when her brother came into the room.

'I thought you'd gone. The post came. Nothing interesting.'

Grant picked up the letters from the table below the mirror. 'I was downstairs. Bel, your room's above Karen's – did you hear anything last night?'

She smoothed a lock of blonde hair into place. 'No, why?'

'Karen thinks someone broke into her room during the night.'

'Burglars?'

'She says that whoever it was tried to smother her with a cushion.'

'Oh, for goodness' sake! What is it with that woman? She seems to thrive on being the centre of a drama!'

24

'That's not Karen's style.'

Belinda shot him a contemptuous glance. 'You're not telling me that you believe her?'

'She looked pretty rattled this morning.'

'Of course she did – she had you for an audience.'

'Belinda, why have you never liked Karen?'

'Oh, does it show?' His sister's voice was heavy with sarcasm. 'Well, for a start, look at what she's done to you.'

'It takes two to marry. We both made a mistake and we're not bitter about it. It was as much my fault as Karen's.'

'I know you, Grant. I know when you're avoiding facing up to issues.'

'What sort of issues?'

'The truth about your precious wife, for one. When the two of you split up it was poor little Karen everyone felt sorry for, wasn't it? You were only the outsider, like me. She loved all that sympathy and she probably missed it when her precious friends decided to get back to their own lives; then it all came flooding back when some opportunist tramp gave her a bang on the head – though if you ask me, he probably knocked her against the wall accidentally while he was trying to get away in a panic. And now that *that* little bit of excitement has died down,' Belinda surged on, her lovely face flushed with spite, 'here she comes again with some story about intruders.'

Grant tapped the letters against his other hand, frowning. 'It's not like Karen to make things up, or to imagine them.'

'Oh really? You're all blinkered when it comes to Karen. She's been spoiled all her life. Anything she wants she takes.'

'Bel . . .'

'First she gets engaged to Leigh, then she dumps him for you . . . and now she's got her eye on him again!'

'Is that what this outburst is about – Leigh?'

Belinda coloured. 'Don't be ridiculous!'

'You've got your own eye on him.'

'Karen has no right – she's already dropped him once. She'll probably do it again, when someone new comes along. She's a spoiled brat.'

25

He leaned against the wall, surveying her with a mixture of irritation and amusement. 'You're a fine one to talk, little sister. You grew up with me and Mum and Dad all doting on you. And that husband of yours worshipped you as well.'

She shot a furious glance at him. 'At first, perhaps, but he soon changed. And losing Mummy and Daddy so suddenly . . .' Her face suddenly crumpled. 'How could you compare what's happened to me with what's happened to *her*?' she wailed.

'Oh, I'm sorry, Bel.' He could never stand seeing his younger sister in tears. Now he patted her shoulder. 'I was just teasing. I shouldn't have said that.'

'No, you shouldn't.'

'It's just . . . I think you're being too hard on Karen. You don't really know her . . .'

'I know that she only married you because you were essential to her father's precious business, then when she was bored with you she dropped you.' She put a hand on his arm. 'And I can't bear to see you being hurt.'

'That's nonsense.' Grant twitched his arm away from beneath the light caress. 'It takes two to end a marriage, Belinda. I haven't got any hang-ups about what happened, and neither does Karen.'

'But you're still here.'

'I care as much about Fletcher and Company as Karen does . . . as Dan did, come to that. It's the business that keeps me here, not Karen.'

'Still under her roof,' his sister persisted, her green eyes narrowing.

'This flat was only going to lie empty. I pay full rent for it.'

'I'm sure she made certain of that.'

'We both did. Doesn't that prove that there's no bitterness between us?'

'If you say so.' Belinda picked up her bag and brushed past him. 'I'd better go or I'll be late. Oh . . . tell Leigh I won't be able to meet him for lunch until quarter past, will you? Someone's coming in during her lunch hour to see a house, and I have to show her around.'

'Lunch with Leigh again?' Grant teased.

'Again.' His sister flashed a tight smile at him. 'I've decided that if Karen wants him back, she'll have to fight for him.'

'Hang on,' he remembered to say as she was leaving. 'You've not seen Monty this morning, have you?'

'No, why?'

'He's gone missing.'

'So he's going to be Karen's next drama, is he?'

'For heaven's sake, Belinda!'

'Have a nice day,' she said, and went.

As always, the flat was calmer without her brittle presence. Grant wandered into the well-appointed kitchen, put water in the kettle, and spooned coffee powder into a cup, wondering why his sister never seemed to be able to relax. Even as a tiny child she had clung to their parents, demanding attention from them and from Grant – attention that was willingly given, for there was something about Belinda that made them all want to guard her from the harsh realities of life.

They hadn't always managed to do that, especially when she had fallen deeply and suddenly in love before her twentieth birthday. Within months of meeting George Solomon she had married him, and gone off with him to Canada, radiantly happy and on the threshold, as she had said at the time, of the life she had always wanted. But nothing that Belinda ever got turned out to be what she really wanted. Her marriage had turned sour, and she had immediately rushed home – only, now that their parents were no longer there, home was wherever Grant was.

'Just the two of us, against the rest of the world,' she had said when she moved into the flat. 'I'm going to look after you, Grant; I promise you that.'

That, Grant thought, was debatable. He carried the coffee into the living room and stood staring out of the window at the broad sweep of lawn, surrounded on all sides by trees. Dan Fletcher had loved trees and the privacy they gave him and his household.

After a while he went back to the kitchen to empty the coffee, untasted, down the sink.

Four

Monty didn't come back and, despite every effort to publicise his disappearance, nobody seemed to have seen him. Pressured by Joyce and Anna into taking things quietly for the next two days, Karen missed the little dog's company more and more.

On the third day of her being left alone in the house, the boredom became unbearable. Leaving a brief note for Joyce, she took her car from the large garage at the rear of the house and drove through the town to the house where Forbes and Charlie Leslie lived.

Charlie answered the door, wearing a man's shirt, large and streaked with paint, over a pair of shabby jeans.

'Karen!' Her hug was warm and genuine. 'Come in – how lovely to see you!'

'You're still working. I should have phoned ahead to make sure it was all right.'

'No, you shouldn't. I'd got to the stage where I was tempted to keep on fussing over that last painting – never a good idea. Best to call it a day and let the thing take its own chances.' Charlie led the way into the sitting room, cluttered as usual with the debris necessary for four people, two adults and two children, all leading busy lives. 'I'm so glad to see you.' She pushed dark hair back from her round face, peering at Karen. 'So . . . how are you?'

'Bored, and tired of Joyce's fussing.'

'Forbes said that your Monty had gone AWOL. Is he back?'

'There's not a sign of him so far. I can't understand it; he's never disappeared like this before.'

'Mmmm. And there's hardly a soul round here who wouldn't recognise him. But not to worry,' Charlie added in an obvious attempt to cheer her friend up, 'he's probably out womanising. He'll come back when he's good and ready. D'you want a coffee here, or in the Silver Teapot?'

'Let's go out,' said Karen, who knew from experience that her best friend was not good at making coffee.

'Wise choice. I've got to go out to the shops anyway. There's scarcely a crumb of food in the house and the children always come home from school starving. I don't know why; the school dinners seem to be substantial enough. Give me a moment to change and get rid of the paint from under my fingernails.'

While she waited, Karen wandered into Charlie's studio, a small extension at the rear of the house. She loved the room with its smell of paint and linseed oil and turps, and the casual clutter of canvases and sketch pads. Charlie had been the star of their school art classes, and she had gone on to art college while Karen, at her father's insistence, had spent a year at a finishing school.

'One day,' Charlie said from the doorway, 'I must get this place organised. The trouble is, I know that if I do that, I'll never find anything again.'

'You look wonderful.'

'And you're a flatterer.' Most women fretted about being slim, but Charlie had allowed motherhood and contentment to develop her already sturdy figure. She even emphasised her shape by wearing patterns and bright colours. Today she wore an orange-patterned top over loose red trousers, her long dark hair was tied back with a scarlet scarf, and her face shone with soap, water and good health.

She winked. 'If you've got it, kid, then why not flaunt it?'

'Oops, look who's here,' Charlie said as they went into the Silver Teapot. Glancing in the direction of her nod, Karen saw Grant and Edith Carpenter at a small corner table, absorbed in conversation. Before Karen could stop her, Charlie was pushing her way towards them.

30

'Fancy seeing you two. Playing truant?' she was asking, as Karen arrived by her side.

For once Edith seemed to be lost for words, but Grant said easily, as he got to his feet, 'We just felt like a change. It's good to get out of the office sometimes. I would ask you to join us, but . . .' He gestured at the small table.

'It's all right; we're here for a gossip ourselves,' Karen told him.

'No sign of Monty yet?'

'Not yet; I'm beginning to think that . . .' She broke off, and Charlie squeezed her arm.

'He'll be back,' she said firmly, and Grant nodded.

'I'm sure he will, Karen.'

'Let's hope so. There's a table over there, Charlie. We'd best go before someone else takes it.'

'Now why would they come here for coffee instead of having it in the office?' Charlie wondered aloud as they settled at their table.

'You heard Grant: they just wanted a change.'

'Judging by the way the two of them had their heads close together when we came in, they must have something very confidential to talk about.' Charlie's eyes were bright with interest. 'They've been seen together quite a lot recently.'

'Have they?'

Charlie had always enjoyed gossip, even at school. 'I think it started when you were in the hospital. He's even been seen – and don't the gossips love it . . .' Charlie broke off as the waitress arrived to take their order.

When she had gone, Karen probed. 'You were saying that Grant had been seen . . . ?'

'Oh yes. Someone saw him going into Edith's flat.'

Karen looked suitably shocked. 'And him a married man, too!'

'Well, everyone knows that you and Grant are history.'

'True.'

'And that Leigh's desperate to marry you.'

'Now you're beginning to sound like Joyce.' Karen made a

31

face. 'She can't wait to see me settled down with Leigh, but I've already let him down once and I'd hate to do it again, Charlie. He deserves better and I don't think I'm very good at marriage.'

'Nonsense. You and Grant rushed into it, and that's probably why it didn't work out. He had only come to the town months before you got engaged, whereas Leigh had been working for your father for a year, at least, before he proposed.'

'A case of "Marry in haste, repent at leisure"?' Karen asked. 'It's true. I really thought when I said yes to Leigh that I loved him and wanted to live with him for the rest of my life. But Grant . . .' she hesitated, frowning. 'With him, the mutual attraction was so immediate, so exciting, that I didn't want to stop and think. It was a roller-coaster experience, and it came off the rails.'

'But you had fun while it lasted?'

'Oh yes, we both had fun. Though it never would have lasted.' Karen came back to earth with a bump. 'And that's why I don't want to rush into anything with Leigh. One mistake is forgivable, but not two. I've learned my lesson.'

'Perhaps Grant has too. I don't see someone as well-controlled as Edith allowing herself to be swept off her feet,' Charlie said, and then hesitated. 'Me talking about Grant and Edith being seen around together doesn't bother you, does it?'

'Not in the least.'

'I just wondered, because Edith seemed a bit disconcerted at seeing you just now. Though perhaps the gossips have got it wrong this time. I mean, there must be quite an age-gap. How old is Edith anyway?'

'I don't know.' Karen tried to do sums in her head. 'She's been with the company for as long as I can remember, and I know that she was in her teens when she first started. That probably puts her in her mid-forties now. And Grant's thirty-five, seven years older than me. Ten years isn't that much of an age-difference these days, and you have to admit, Charlie, that Edith is very attractive.'

'Mmmm, if you like that look of superefficiency. Thank goodness my Forbes doesn't mind being married to someone who muddles her way through life.'

The waitress arrived with their order, and Charlie stirred sugar into her coffee then bit into a chocolate eclair. 'Mmm, lovely. Very good for energy, you know. Where were we? Oh yes, you and your legion of admirers. I remember going through hell once over you and Forbes.'

'What?'

'It's true.' Charlie licked a stray dollop of cream from the tip of a finger. 'Remember when I was at art school and you were at finishing school, and we only saw the old crowd in the holidays? The boys hovered around you, while I just came in handy if they needed someone to umpire tennis matches, or be silly mid-off or whatever it was called if they didn't have a sufficient number to make up a cricket team. Good old Charlie, one of the boys. It didn't bother me a bit until all of a sudden I fell madly in love with Forbes . . . only he didn't have eyes for anyone but you.'

Karen gaped at her. Forbes was only dimly remembered from those days as an inarticulate youth, hanging around on the fringe of the group. Then he had married Charlie, and under her wing he had learned self-confidence and was now a valuable and capable member of the Fletcher team. She could not imagine him as a prospective suitor. 'But I never encouraged Forbes!'

'You didn't have to. Just being there was enough. It seemed so unfair at the time – you having a doting father and all that money behind you, and gorgeous looks as well,' Charlie said thoughtfully. 'I hated you more than a little, that summer.'

'Oh, Charlie!'

'Tush, girl, don't look so guilty! It's all in the past. Leigh came on the scene, you fell for him and I got Forbes. On the rebound, admittedly, but I got him. And he's over that crush on you, by the way,' she added solemnly. 'We've been very happy together and I'm still crazy about him, even though his hair's slipping a bit. Do you remember . . .' She changed the subject, leading the two of them down memory lane. It was half an hour before Charlie pushed her empty coffee cup away.

'I suppose I must gather in a sheaf or two to keep my brood free from the threat of malnutrition; then it's home to get that dratted painting sorted out.' She beamed at Karen. 'Hasn't this been lovely?'

'We must do it more often.' As she followed Charlie out of the tearoom, Karen saw that Grant and Edith were still there, still talking earnestly, oblivious to everyone else.

Following Charlie round the shops, Karen felt envious as she watched her friend buying meat and vegetables, trying to decide between cabbages and cauliflowers. Suddenly, being a housewife with a hungry family to feed seemed much more desirable than being the local symbol of industry. Sometimes, she thought as Charlie collected her change and made some laughing remark to the shop assistant before turning away from the counter, she felt so useless.

'We're hoping to take some time off the week after next,' Charlie said as they drove back to her house. 'Forbes is due a few days' holiday and his mother's offered to move in and look after the boys. We're going to get away from it all . . . find a nice quiet little hotel somewhere and get to know each other ag— Look out!' she yelled as a small black dog rushed on to the road, almost under the car wheels.

They were both thrown against their seat belts as Karen braked, her mouth dry. Monty – it was Monty! But as she wound down her window to call his name, the dog gained the opposite pavement and began to dance about a harassed woman with a little girl in tow.

'Bruno!' The woman caught hold of his collar then called over to the car, 'I'm so sorry; he doesn't usually behave so badly.'

'It's all right. As long as he's OK.' Karen wound the window up again and started the car.

'Are you all right?' Charlie asked. 'You went as white as a sheet there.'

'I'm fine. Look . . . why don't you and Forbes use the cottage . . . if you don't mind doing your own cooking, that is.'

'D'you mean it? That would be lovely!'

'Of course I mean it. Tell you what: if you're free on Friday we could drive over to find out what sort of mess the police have left it in.'

'Would it bother you, going back there?' Charlie asked cautiously.

'Not with you there as well. I need a day out, and I need to see the place again.'

'Like getting on a horse right after a fall?'

'Exactly. I've been wondering if going back there might help me to remember more about what happened, but I wouldn't want to go alone,' Karen admitted.

'Lightning doesn't strike twice in the same place. And it isn't the cottage's fault that you got hurt there,' Charlie said firmly. 'It must hold a lot of happy memories for you.'

'It does. My father and I had some wonderful times there.' But it wasn't her father Karen thought of as she spoke. Grant had proposed to her at the cottage and part of their honeymoon had been spent there.

'It'll certainly be fun, you and me off on our own together,' Charlie said as the car stopped at her gate. 'Like being kids again. See you on Friday morning.'

As Karen drove off Charlie's casual words echoed in her mind: 'I hated you more than a little, that summer.'

It had never occurred to her, in those golden days, that her best friend resented her popularity. Now, just when she was trying to cope with the suspicion that someone might, for some unknown reason, hate her enough to try to kill her, Charlie's revelation was like a slap in the face.

Although her mother had died when she herself was only just beginning to toddle, Karen had enjoyed a childhood lapped in love and security. Joyce and Anna had raised her between them and Dan Fletcher, busy though he was, always had time for his beloved daughter. Karen had shared all his free time and, as she grew older, there had been no shortage of friends.

Life had been perfect, but perhaps the time had come, she thought as she drove home, to put something back instead of taking all the time. Her father had never had a son to follow him into the business, but there was no reason why his daughter shouldn't get more involved in it.

Tomorrow, she promised herself, she would make a start.

A visit from the head of the company always surprised the employees. It was so rarely that Karen drove through the gates, except for a board meeting, that she received curious stares from the men and women who were leaving for their midday meal.

Steering the car cautiously through the crowd, she wondered what they thought about her – if they ever thought about her at all. Her father had known every single one of his employees and had taken an interest in their families too; she recalled him talking about them, but she had always been too caught up in her own interests to listen properly. As a result, she herself knew nothing about those people. That, she decided as she parked the car and went into the office, would have to change.

The first person she ran into – literally – was Grant, who hurried, head down, round a corner as she turned it from the opposite direction. She staggered under the impact and might have fallen if he hadn't caught her arms.

'Sorry, I . . . Karen, what are you doing here?'

'I have an interest in the place, remember?'

He knelt to pick up the sheaf of papers that had fallen in the collision. 'You always had. Why the visit now . . . or has a special board meeting been called?' he added, sudden suspicion in his open face. 'If it has, I've not been told about it.'

'There's no meeting, I've just decided that I should spend more time here, and learn something about the business,' she said self-consciously, then felt herself colour as he looked at her with sudden interest.

'If you really mean that, you could start right now. In here . . .' They were near the boardroom and now he ushered her in. 'I'll be back in a minute, so don't go away,' he ordered, and hurried out again.

Five

G rant was gone for some time, and while she waited for him Karen wandered to the large window running down one wall. It looked out on to a central courtyard; directly opposite, she could see the big building that housed the machines where the cloth was manufactured. And here – she turned to look at it – in this very room, the crucial decisions were made and controversial views thrashed out. Since her father's death she had been present at those meetings without really listening to a word that had been said.

'Fletcher women don't need to bother with business,' Dan had always told her. 'I see to all that.'

With no sons of his own to follow him into the company, he had been on the lookout for ambitious, hardworking young men who could be trained to become his assistants. Leigh, a university graduate from London, had been the first. Dan had encouraged and groomed him until Leigh won himself a strong position in the firm – and in Karen's heart. Then Grant, who lived in a nearby town, had come along. He too was hardworking and capable, and soon he had become as important to the firm as Leigh already was. Two young assistants, one to run the office and the other to look after the factory when he retired, suited Dan very well; but he had not been so pleased when his daughter fell head over heels in love with Grant. The one and only quarrel between father and daughter had been caused by her love for Grant Roberts, for, much as he liked Grant, Dan had been furious with what he saw as his daughter's fickle behaviour.

It was Leigh himself who had done a lot to heal the breach

between father and daughter, pointing out to Dan that he had no intention of marrying a reluctant bride. And so Karen and Grant had married with Leigh's blessing as well as Dan's.

Karen bit her lip as she remembered their lavish, fairy-tale social wedding, followed by an idyllic honeymoon before they had returned to live in the upper flat of the Fletcher house. Grant had wanted to buy a home of their own, but Karen and Dan, who had spent a fortune on altering the upper floor for them, had won the argument.

Leigh, who had bought the house next door when he and Karen had been engaged, was their closest friend, and Karen was blissfully happy – for a while.

When their marriage began to crumble she had blamed Grant for being too pig-headed, too absorbed in the firm, too stubborn. Now, with the clear-sightedness she had developed during her enforced convalescence after the accident, she felt that perhaps the immaturity had been hers, rather than his.

For Dan's sake they had kept up pretence of happiness, then one terrible day he had collapsed at his desk and died on the way to hospital. It was only later that they discovered he had been having treatment for a heart ailment for almost a year.

He had organised his affairs efficiently, leaving shares in the business to Edith, Grant and Leigh, with Karen holding the major portion. Joyce had been left a token number of shares in acknowledgement of her rights as a Fletcher, although Dan had specified that if Karen should die childless, her majority shares would go to Joyce, in order to keep them within the family.

Six months later Karen and Grant had ended the storm-tossed, bickering mess their marriage had become. Since there was no question of Grant, a shareholder and works manager, leaving the company, Karen had simply moved herself and her belongings downstairs, leaving him and, ultimately, Belinda, in the flat that had been her father's wedding gift to them.

'Sorry about that – I was waylaid.' Grant hurried in and dropped a thick folder on to the table. 'Karen – how are you, by the way?' he added as an afterthought.

'Me? Oh, I'm fine now. In fact . . .' Seeing his eyes on the sticking plaster that still decorated her forehead, she reached up and, finding a loose corner, gave it a sharp tug. 'Ow!' She rubbed her stinging skin and then asked, 'How does it look?'

'There's a scar.' He reached out to touch it with the tip of a finger; then, when Karen instinctively took a step back, his hand fell to his side. 'Sorry, I shouldn't have . . .'

'It's all right,' she said awkwardly, furious with herself. Now he would think that she couldn't bear to be touched by him, when in actual fact she was still awash with memories, and feeling vulnerable. Once, his touch had made her feel as though she was melting inside.

She tossed the lint and plaster into a waste-paper bucket, glad of the chance to turn away from him and compose herself.

'No more memories?' he asked when she turned back to face him; then, when she shook her head, 'That's probably for the best, given the situation.'

'What situation?'

'The wound being on your forehead, near the temple.'

For a long moment she stared blankly, then realised what he meant. All these weeks she had assumed, for some reason, that her assailant had come up behind her.

'I must have seen it coming,' she said at last, in a whisper. 'I must have seen . . . his face . . .'

'Karen? God, I'm sorry, I didn't stop to think – here, sit down.' He pulled out a chair, but she shook her head and took a long, deep breath.

'I'm fine. It's just that I hadn't thought about . . . of course . . . Grant, I saw whoever did this!'

'Only for a second or so,' he told her swiftly. 'That's why it's best to leave things as they are. It'll save any unpleasant memories, not to mention identity parades and so forth. Not that the police seem to have any leads as yet.'

'You've heard from them recently?'

'I keep in touch with them. You're still my wife, until such time as we decide to cut the knot legally, and I don't have to be happily married to you to care about your welfare . . .' He stopped, cleared his throat, then added with a lift of one eyebrow, 'And you're my boss as well as my landlady, so your welfare is mine too, OK? Now . . .' He opened the folder and began to spill blueprints and sketches across the table. 'I wanted to talk to you about this idea of Ramsay's . . . He only came into the firm recently, but he's good, Karen. Dan would have appreciated him. He's come up with a new idea for a different kind of cloth – but in order to produce it we'll need to bring in new machinery.'

'Can't the existing machinery handle it?'

'Not a chance.' Grant launched into a string of technical reasons, which Karen tried hard to follow. She tried to come up with an intelligent thought, and finally, when he paused for breath, ventured, 'Would it be possible to modify some of the machinery we've got just now?'

'Clever girl – you've got more of a business mind than you let on. As a matter of fact, it might just be possible. It's one of the points I want to put before the next meeting.'

'But I thought that Leigh was already opposed to this idea because of cost, and didn't Forbes say that we have a full order book just now?'

'They're being short-sighted!' Grant broke in impatiently. 'Karen, you're Dan's daughter; try to put yourself in his place for a minute! If he was still here I know that he'd back me on this. If we bring out this new cloth we could corner the market, but we'll have to act now, not wait until we have nothing better to do. It's only a matter of time before some other firm beats us to it. Talented young designers are in demand just now and I can't expect Mike Ramsay to cool his heels until Leigh and Forbes decide to listen to him. He'll resign and take his idea elsewhere – that's certainly what I'd do if I were in his shoes.'

He paced the floor as he talked, the words pouring out. 'Yes, we could modify some of the machinery we already have, but Leigh will probably turn that idea down on the grounds that it would take too much time and money and tie up machines that could be doing other work. But it would be worth the risk, Karen! I know that, but I can't get it through their heads! I don't know what it is with Leigh these days; anyone would think that *he* owned the company, and not you.'

'I might own it, but you and Leigh and Edith know a lot more about it than I do.'

'You're the chairwoman. You've got clout.'

'Not much of a chairwoman. I haven't done one single, useful thing since I took over.'

'So now's your chance. You told me that you wanted to take more of an interest in things, didn't you?'

Karen bit her lip. 'Grant, I don't feel happy about taking sides in a disagreement between you and Leigh.'

His eyes darkened with impatience. It was a look she well knew. 'Either he gets his way in this, or I get mine. Someone has to win and someone has to lose. You can't sit on the fence as far as this argument's concerned.' Then, before she could reply, 'Or are you reluctant to alienate Leigh, since he's going to be your next husband?'

'What makes you think that?'

'We all know the way the wind's blowing.'

'So now you listen to gossip?'

'I don't need to listen, I know you.'

'What makes you think that I'd ever want to marry again after the experience I went through with you?'

'Of course you do. You need to have a man around, Karen; you always have. First it was Daddy, then me, and it's obvious that the next one will be Leigh. You're not adult enough to be on your own for long.'

He had said the wrong thing. Sudden memories of the final, tumultuous days of their marriage, of Grant bawling at her, 'When will you ever grow up?' swept in on Karen, and she felt herself stiffen.

'That's typical: one minute you're begging for my help and the next minute you're insulting me. Well, you can get Edith to help you, because I certainly won't.'

'What does Edith have to do with anything?'

'You tell me – you certainly seemed to be very close the other day in the tearoom.'

He looked at her for a long moment, familiar storm clouds gathering in his eyes. 'Still the same prickly, don't-criticise-me-my-name's-Fletcher Karen, aren't you?'

'That name has done a lot for you, remember?'

'As if I could ever forget. That's what killed our marriage,' he flashed back at her. 'Morning, noon and night, that constant reminder that it was you and your father who had put me where I was. How could any man survive a marriage like that? Yes, Dan Fletcher gave me my big chance in life, and I'll be eternally grateful to him for that. Dan was a god to the people round here, but he was human too, human enough to cope with the adulation. He was one of us. He worked damned hard; and I've seen him down in that mill, operating a machine when he had to. He didn't believe in lording it in a plush office – not Dan Fletcher.' Then, his tone changing from respect to contempt: 'But you – you might be a Fletcher, and you might be Dan's daughter, but you've not earned the right to ride roughshod over me or anyone else!'

'Perhaps if my father had been married to you, as I was, he would have changed his opinion of you!'

It had only taken a few careless words to dredge up the old enmity between them. Now they glared at each other across the table.

'Perhaps you're right,' Grant said coolly. 'But he wasn't married to me, and you are, sweetheart. And that means that your name's not Fletcher any more. It's Roberts, and I wish I'd insisted on you remembering that!'

Karen swept the papers from the table with a furious, childish gesture. 'It won't be Roberts for long. That was a mistake that I can erase from the records . . . and I will, as soon as I can!'

Grant looked from her face to the papers scattered about the floor. When he spoke, his voice was quiet and controlled, although his face was a mask, wiped clean of expression. 'There's something else I should have done. I should have knocked the pride out of you as soon as you started throwing your weight around, instead of trying to tolerate your spoiled temper. Who knows – I might have managed to turn you into a real woman!'

Karen opened her mouth to retaliate and then closed it again, turning instead to storm from the room.

Once in the corridor, she discovered that she was shaking violently. Since agreeing to end their marriage she and Grant had carefully avoided further confrontation and had succeeded in maintaining a civilised, if slightly reserved, friendship. Five minutes ago, listening to him talk about the new project, she had dared to hope that they had finally settled their differences; it was frightening now to realise that they were still capable of such wounding bitterness towards each other.

She wandered aimlessly along the corridor, and then paused as Leigh hailed her from his office. 'Karen?' Then, as she turned back towards the open door, 'This is a lovely surprise. Come on in.'

Still bruised by Grant's criticism, she hesitated. 'Are you busy?'

'Never too busy for you.' He got up and came round his desk to kiss her and draw her into the room. 'What brings you here?'

'Just an impulse.'

'You should have them more often.'

'I might just do that. As a matter of fact, I've decided that I should work harder at running Fletcher and Company.'

Leigh's expressive eyebrows tucked together. 'Aren't you satisfied with the job we do?'

'Very satisfied, but I feel like a drone. Would you – could you teach me about the business?'

'Why not?' He studied her with open admiration. 'You look like good executive material to me. Now then, the first thing you have to learn to do is be nice to the office manager.'

'Who just happens to be you.'

'Pure coincidence. Have dinner with me tonight.'

'I don't know, Leigh . . . I'm still not up to socialising.'

'Who mentioned socialising? Just an early dinner, some-where relaxing. We can go straight from here if you want.

44

I'll phone Joyce to let her know that you'll be back mid-evening.'

'It might be just what I need.'

'That's what I think. You were upset when you came in here, weren't you? What happened?'

She shrugged. 'Nothing much. I met Grant when I arrived, and we had one of our . . . disagreements.'

'For God's sake!' Leigh exploded, 'is he trying to give you a relapse? I sometimes think that he – what was it about?'

'Nothing in particular, like most of our rows. Let's forget it.' She summoned up a smile. 'I came here to learn about the business, remember?'

'So you did. Now then . . .' He went back to the desk and drew up another chair. 'Take a seat, madam, and we'll start with a brief run-down on the successful secrets of Fletcher and Company.'

Six

They had dinner in a small family restaurant on the outskirts of town. Because it was early the place was quiet and, as the meal progressed, Karen felt her anxieties drift away. Leigh was so easy to be with: there was a comforting maturity about him; although he was thirty years old – two years older than she was herself but five years younger than Grant – she had always felt that the two men in her life were much of an age. Perhaps it was Leigh's strong sense of ambition that made him seem older than he was.

His manner also reminded her frequently of her father, another man who had given the impression of always being eager to push his way forward towards new frontiers. Grant, on the other hand, had been capable and hardworking, but his ambitions were hidden below a laid-back attitude and only came to the surface on special occasions, like that afternoon, when he was trying to get her to understand the importance of Mike Ramsay's new material. But as ever, their discussion had turned into an argument, proving yet again that they should never have got married.

Why, she wondered, looking across the table at Leigh, had she been so stupid, and broken off her engagement to him? It had been an act of madness, and now she regretted it with all her heart. It took a moment to realise that he was leaning forward, smiling at her, waiting for a reply to something he had just said.

'Sorry . . . what?'

'I said, a penny for your thoughts. I had been talking about Fletcher's, then I realised that you were miles away.'

46

'Oh . . . I'm not very good at concentrating in the evenings.' She put a hand to her forehead and was surprised to find that her fingertips encountered skin instead of the plaster that had been there.

'I'm not surprised. I have been going on a bit. Why don't you come over to the house tomorrow evening? We can work on the business angle in comfort then.'

'Tomorrow's Friday – I'm going to the cottage with Charlie. It's all right,' she added hurriedly as he frowned slightly and began to say something, 'I want to go. I need to see the place again, and I won't be on my own. Charlie and Forbes are planning to spend a few days there, and I have to make sure that it's ready for them. But I'll be back home later in the afternoon, so I could come across after dinner.'

'Fine.'

'Leigh,' she asked on an impulse, 'did it occur to you that I must have seen my attacker?'

'Why on earth bring that up now?'

'Grant mentioned it.'

'Why the hell did he have to mention what happened at the cottage? We all agreed to let that subject drop . . . he should have known better.'

'Why shouldn't he talk to me about it?'

'Because it still upsets you.'

'But I need to know what happened. Until he mentioned it I hadn't realised . . . for some reason I had assumed that whoever it was had come at me from behind. It means that I might be able to identify him, if I got my memory back.'

'And if they ever find him, which is unlikely at this late stage.'

'What . . .' Karen began, but the words caught in her throat. She swallowed hard, and then tried again. 'What if it turned out to be someone I knew?'

A smile tugged at the corner of his mouth. 'You travel extensively among burglars and criminals?'

'Don't joke about it! I don't think anything was taken from

the cottage, was it? That means that it might not have been a burglar.'

'Of course it was . . . or a tramp looking for food, and perhaps some shelter for the night.' A slight impatience began to creep into his voice. 'You disturbed him and he lashed out in a panic, then ran away when he realised what he'd done. Come to think of it, didn't your handbag disappear?'

'I'd forgotten about that. My name and my address were in that bag.' About to take a sip of wine, she put the glass down untasted. 'He knows who I am. He could have found out that I recovered – he might be afraid that I would remember. Leigh, he might have come to the house the other night to . . .'

'To what?' Leigh asked sharply, and she realised that he knew nothing of the fright she had got in the night.

'Nothing, it was just a bad dream I had . . .'

'Don't lie to me, Karen. Something happened and I want to know what it was!'

She had no option but to tell him, as briefly as possible.

'Why did nobody tell me?' he wanted to know when she had finished.

'We all wanted to forget it. I told you, it was probably just a nightmare. Grant looked outside the next morning, and there was no trace . . .'

'Roberts knew about this?'

'He dropped in on Anna the next morning; you know he does that often. And of course Joyce told him the whole story.'

'He should have insisted on contacting the police. We should do that now.' His voice had risen slightly and she noticed that the waiters and the few people sharing the restaurant were glancing over. She put a hand on his.

'Leigh, I have no proof that there really was someone in my room. It's over and done with now. Let's leave it at that.'

'I'll leave it if you'll accept this, Karen . . .' He turned the hand she covered, so that it trapped hers, holding it tightly. 'Whoever was at the cottage that day is far away now.'

'How do you know that?' Tension made her voice rise. 'How can I be sure of it?'

48

'He'd not be likely to hang about, would he? He would have got right out of the area before the police started snooping around. You'll never hear from him or see him again,' Leigh said firmly. 'And now, I think I should take you home: you look tired.'

She nodded. 'I am. And I've got my own car outside, but you can walk me to it, if you want.'

'Why don't you leave your car here?' he suggested in the car park. 'Then I can drive you home and bring you back to collect it tomorrow.'

'Certainly not. I'm well able to drive myself.'

'Are you sure?'

'Don't fuss, Leigh; I'm a big girl now.'

'I know that, but I . . . I care about you,' he said, his voice thickening. 'I care just as much as I did that day when I asked you to marry me. Remember?'

'How could I forget?' On an impulse, she drew his head down to hers and kissed him. 'Oh Leigh, I'm so sorry.'

'For what?'

'For breaking off our engagement. For treating you so badly.'

He held her loosely within the circle of his arms. 'You fell for Grant, and decided that you wanted him more than you wanted me.'

'That,' Karen said wryly, 'was the biggest mistake I ever made.'

'We all make mistakes. It's the only way we can learn. And once we've learned we never make them again. So . . .' They kissed again, a long deep kiss that sent tingles to the tips of her toes. '. . . when are you going to divorce Grant and marry me?' he murmured when they finally drew apart.

It would have been so easy to commit herself there and then, to let him take charge and look after her; but she knew that, while she was carrying so much excess emotional baggage, it would be a mistake to yield to temptation. If . . . when . . . she married again she wanted it to be perfect, and for ever.

49

'Give me time, Leigh . . . please? I still feel like . . . I still feel incomplete.'

He laughed, and dropped a kiss on her nose. 'I think you're very complete.'

'With a block of my life blotted out?' she started to say, and then the words were smothered by his fingertips.

'Stop it, Karen. Stop fretting about that.' Then, with a laugh, 'And may I say that you chose a hell of a way to fob off a proposal!'

'Just because I don't want to make a commitment now,' Karen said into his jacket, 'it doesn't mean that I don't want you to keep trying.'

'Good. And remember, if you ever need me I'm only a phone call away.'

'My knight in shining armour?'

'You can rely on that, always,' he said, and she surprised herself by tightening her grip on him and burying her face in his shoulder.

'Leigh, don't ever give up on me!'

'As if I ever would,' he murmured into her hair. 'As if I ever could!'

The talk with Leigh had done her good, and on the way home Karen's spirits were high. On the passenger seat by her side lay a thick folder, which she intended to study in detail. At last, she was going to be more than just a symbol, a name.

Her hands tightened on the wheel as she wondered what it would be like to work alongside Grant. If she were going to spend more time in the office, they would have to learn to treat each other as colleagues and forget their former emotional ties; she could start by seeking him out soon and asking him to tell her more about the new material that excited him so much.

The driveway, which curled round the house to the huge garage at the back, was always well lit, and Karen took the car right round instead of leaving it out all night. Joyce didn't drive, but Grant's and Belinda's cars were already in for the night. She took the folder Leigh had given her from the back seat and tucked it under her arm before leaving the garage, clicking the remote control and hearing the automatic door close at her back. She couldn't wait to start work on the folder. At last she was going to bring some routine into her life.

Smiling, she opened the door and went into the large, comfortable kitchen. Then the smile faded as she saw the three woman there: Anna, even more grim-faced than usual; Joyce, looking strangely pale, and Helen, the maid, with her hands at her mouth and her eyes sparkling with tears.

'Oh, Mrs Roberts,' the girl choked. 'He was such a sweet wee dog!'

'Monty?' Karen felt the blood drain from her face. 'Where is he?'

'In one of the outhouses, and you'd be best staying here,' Anna said; but Karen was already turning, surging to the door.

Grant stood there, blocking her way, standing firm when she tried to push past him.

'Leave it, Karen.'

'What happened?'

'A farmhand brought him back half an hour ago,' Grant said. 'He was found in one of the fields. It looks as though he might have been poisoned.'

'No!'

'I'm sorry,' Grant said. 'Karen, I'm so sorry.'

For the sake of privacy, the garden was bordered on all sides by shrubbery, mainly tall rhododendrons that, in early summer, carried white, pink, crimson and purple blossoms the size of dinner plates. The shrubbery was at its thickest between the house and the road, with two or three clearings. The old summer house where Karen had played with her dolls as a child was in one clearing, and in another, where the bushes were augmented by tall trees, various family pets had been buried. Here, early the next morning, she and Grant laid Monty in his grave. It was a sad occasion for them both; Monty had been a symbol of the love they had once shared and, with his death, it seemed to Karen that a door had clanged shut on the past.

'Why now, after all those years of roaming about the

countryside?' she asked helplessly, watching spadefuls of earth cover the box Grant had found from somewhere.

'He was just unlucky, poor little chap. There are nutters who try to trap or kill vermin and birds of prey – you know that. And sometimes domestic pets find the stuff first, and eat it. Monty may have been fortunate to escape until now.' He finished his work and smoothed the grave's surface with the back of the spade. 'We'll put up a marker once the earth has had time to settle.'

'It's too much of a coincidence, Grant, after the way he disappeared at the cottage, then again the other night when someone was in my room. It's as if someone wanted him out of the way, and now . . .'

'Don't start all that again! You know that I checked all round the outside of the house the next morning, and there was no trace of anyone going in through that French window, or coming out again. It must have been a dream.'

'But . . .' Suddenly Karen was aware of the fact that they were alone in the small clearing, hidden from view by the tall rhododendrons all about. She became aware, too, of the spade held loosely between Grant's hands. She took a step back, away from him, then another . . . and then, her nerve breaking, she turned and ran, fighting her way through the bushes, leaving him on his own.

'Are you sure you want to go ahead with this trip,' Charlie asked doubtfully, 'what with Monty and everything? We can always go another time.'

'I'm sure. Joyce means well, but I can't bear another minute of her silent sympathy, and even though I know he's gone for ever, I can't seem to stop expecting him to come dashing into the room. And . . .' She stopped, on the verge of telling her friend what a fool she had made of herself in front of Grant at the dog's graveside, then changing her mind. 'I've got a heavy weekend ahead, trying to make sense of a bundle of business papers that Leigh's given me. Believe me, this day out is what I most need!'

It was a soft, mellow day, and the route to the cottage, only about fifty miles in all, took them through some glowing autumn countryside. As she drove, Karen felt the tension and the sense of bereavement loosen deep within her and begin to melt away.

'I can recommend this place for evening meals,' she told Charlie as the car passed a small restaurant. 'We . . . I often eat here when I'm at the cottage.'

'Not me . . . I'm going to hole up and sketch and sketch and sketch. And I'm going to take all the time I need over it. Forbes is taking a pile of books, and he's promised to provide the tins and bottles, a tin-opener and paper plates. We're going to hole up, like Mummy and Daddy hibernating bear – with not a cub in sight for once. And Goldilocks will get short shrift if she interrupts us.'

It was early afternoon when they reached the private road that wound up through trees to the house, a small, sturdy building that stood in a clearing. Charlie heaved a sigh of pure pleasure as Karen stopped the car.

'Isn't it lovely? I've not been here for years, but it hasn't changed a bit. We're going to love being here for a whole week,' she enthused, and then, with a sidelong glance, 'How do you feel about seeing it again?'

'It looks fine,' Karen said, surprised. 'Just the way it always has.' She had been secretly afraid of that first glimpse, but the cottage looked so welcoming and so safe that her spirits began to rise. Perhaps this was just what she needed. Perhaps the fears that had niggled at her since the moment she had regained consciousness in the hospital were finally going to be laid to rest.

The interior was stuffy, as was to be expected. Karen pulled off her driving gloves and went to the small lounge to switch on the power and the electric fire while Charlie threw the windows open, declaring, 'At last I really feel as if I'm far away from the rat race!'

Karen prowled about, going into every room, opening and closing drawers and cupboard doors. The place was so normal . . . She was aware of a faint sense of disappointment, realising that, subconsciously, she had hoped that the cottage might in some way give her a clue to what had happened on her last visit.

From the large living-room window she could see Charlie ferreting about in the boot of the car. Taking advantage of her moment's solitude, Karen turned to face the room, trying to reconstruct it the way it had been on the night when she had been attacked. She knew from what she had been told afterwards that she had lit a log fire, and that she had been found lying on the hearthrug. Closing her eyes, she tried to recall the room as it would have looked on that evening. It had been one of the colder summer days and, although it was still light outside, she would have drawn the curtains, as she always did when a log fire blazed in the hearth. Two lamps would have lighted the room, one by the fireside, and the other at the window.

'You weren't attacked from behind,' Grant's voice echoed in her ears. 'You must have seen it coming . . .'

Someone who had come running in from the kitchen after being disturbed? No, because she had had time to unpack the car, fetch the logs and light the fire. Someone who had arrived at the door? Which led to another question: was it somebody she knew, and had welcomed in?

She shivered violently, and was saved from further exploration by Charlie, who burst back into the room with the food hamper.

'I had a look around. There's a huge pile of logs at the side of the house,' she announced with all the excitement of a small child.

'The electric fire's good as far as instant heat is concerned, but there's nothing like curling up in front of a real fire in the evenings.'

'I'll drink to that.' Charlie plunged into the hamper and brought out a bottle and two glasses. 'It's only fizzy white wine, not champagne, but it will do. You've not been told to steer clear of drink by your doctor, have you?'

'No.'

'Pity. If you had been' – Charlie was working on the cork – 'I would have had an excuse to drink your share as well.' She filled the glasses then handed one to Karen. 'A celebration!'

'Of what?'

'Whatever we want. Your recovery, our day out, my forthcoming holiday . . . who says that we need to have a reason? Let's just celebrate!' Then, after sampling the wine: 'Talking about celebrations, when are you and Leigh going to make an announcement?'

Karen choked on her drink and had to be thumped on the back. 'I'm still married to Grant!' she protested when she could speak again.

'But you are going to get divorced, aren't you? And Leigh's crazy about you.' Charlie rushed on when Karen nodded. 'He was in a terrible state when you were so ill and we didn't know which way it was going to go. I don't know if anyone said, but he spent more time by your bedside than anyone, even Joyce.'

'He was the first person I saw when I finally came round. Karen recalled that moment when, dazed and confused, she had opened her eyes to see Leigh's familiar face above her, concern in his dark-blue eyes. She remembered the warmth of his hand on hers, the relief in his face when she had recognised him and managed a wan smile.

'There you are, then. Belinda Solomon did her level best to console him, but he couldn't think of anyone but you.' Charlie lifted the wine bottle, then said, her head cocked to one side, 'You do know that Belinda has her sights set on Leigh?'

'I've noticed. No more for me; I'm ready to eat,' Karen said as Charlie refilled her glass then held the bottle up enquiringly.

'If you don't put him out of his misery soon he might settle for second best, and propose to Belinda. And you don't want that, do you?' Charlie added, leering. 'So get your skates on, girl.'

'To tell you the truth, I don't know what I want at the moment – apart from some food.'

'Coming up.' Charlie bustled into the kitchen. 'Is it too cold to eat out of doors?'

'Not if we keep our coats on. There's a folding table in the back porch, and folding chairs.'

'Let's do it, then, and we can come in by the fire for coffee afterwards. You'll have to get your skates on, my girl.' Charlie prattled on as she unpacked containers and hauled plates and cutlery from the kitchen cupboard. 'You and Leigh will make the perfect couple. Oh, Grant's lovely in a sturdy, rugged sort of way . . . but Leigh's gorgeous. He should have been an actor. There's only one man who looks better than him,' Charlie said, laying everything out on a tray, 'and that's my lovely Forbes.'

Seven

Although the sun was out, there was a chill in the air and they were glad, when they had eaten, to return to the living room, by now well heated, for a leisurely cup of coffee. Then, all too soon, it was time to leave. Charlie dealt with the washing-up while Karen gave the house a final check, closing doors behind her as she went. As she bent to switch off the electric fire she caught sight of a wisp of white almost hidden beneath the fire irons on the hearth. It was a scrap of paper, possibly a bit of envelope, and in small print it carried the words: 'Jopling & C . . .'

She tried hard to think; then, as something began to stir very faintly in the depths of her mind, the room began to swirl about her head. She reached out into empty air in search of something solid to cling to and felt a sharp pain in her fingers as they slammed against the stand holding the fire irons. The noise of the irons falling on to the stone flags brought the room to a sudden, juddering standstill.

'What happened?' Charlie put her head in at the door.

'I just . . .' Karen straightened, then found that her knees were so shaky that she had to sit down in the nearest chair. 'I turned too quickly and it brought on a dizzy spell. I still get them occasionally.'

'You look quite white. Put your head between your knees . . . I'll fetch a glass of water . . .'

'I'm fine, honestly! We'd better be on our way.'

'Not until you've had another cup of coffee and the chance to calm down,' Charlie insisted.

Karen, unable to stay alone in the living room now, went

with her to the kitchen and they drank their coffee at the table there. Then Karen, unable to face returning to the other room, rinsed the mugs while Charlie gathered up their coats.

As she drove down the lane to the road, Karen glanced at the house in the rear-view mirror. It still looked peaceful, but now it seemed, to her, to have a smug air about it as well. Well it might, she thought, for it knew what had happened that night. All at once she knew that she would never be able to go back to it with a light heart. She would have to find somewhere else for those idyllic weekends and impromptu holidays. Then she remembered the scrap of envelope, still lying where she had dropped it, unless Charlie had scooped it up and disposed of it. It didn't matter; she remembered the printing on it vividly.

'Are you sure you're all right, Karen?' Charlie asked. 'Would you like me to drive?'

Remembering her friend's battered little car, and her slapstick way of driving, Karen declined the offer. 'The dizziness has all gone and I'm getting lots of fresh air from this open window. Are you going to the company dance?' she asked with an attempt at cheerfulness.

'Ugh . . . I'd forgotten that.' Charlie grimaced. 'I suppose I'll have to. I hate these things but Forbes insists. I'd much rather he went on his own, but he won't.'

'Of course you must go; you're one of our designers, so you're an important part of the business yourself.'

'I've never liked formal occasions, and it's my mother's fault. She kept forcing me to attend dances and parties – d'you remember? Poor misguided woman, she thought they would suddenly turn me into a nice young lady. Well at least these days I don't have to suffer the humiliation of never being asked to dance. I've got my own partner with me. What about you?'

'I'm going, but I might not stay long. My excuse is that I still can't take too much socialising.'

'You probably shouldn't be there at all.'

'I must put in an appearance. I missed last year's completely, remember?'

'That was understandable: you and Grant had just split up and it would have been an ordeal for you, being the centre of attention. Look at that,' Charlie added with contempt as they passed a long line of hoardings, a splash of gaudy colour against the green fields. 'Monstrosities! I've nothing against advertising, provided it's something clever and attractive; but some of that rubbish is enough to give a driver a sharp attack of nausea and cause an accident.'

Joyce was working in the garden when Karen got home. 'Did you enjoy your day?'

'Every minute of it.'

'Oh, good. How did . . .' Joyce hesitated, her eyes anxious, and then said carefully, 'How was the cottage?'

'It's all right,' Karen assured her aunt; 'there were no bad vibes.'

'So you didn't remember anything?'

The strange feeling that had come over her when she had found the scrap of paper stirred uneasily in the depths of Karen's mind, and was thrust away. 'Not a thing,' she said blithely, and Joyce's face cleared. Then the worried look came back.

'By the way, Belinda has invited us upstairs for coffee after we've eaten.'

'Tonight?' Karen found it hard to keep the dismay from her voice.

'I said we'd go.' Joyce eyed her nervously. 'After all, she doesn't extend invitations very often, and . . . you don't mind, do you?'

'No, but I've arranged to go over to Leigh's after dinner.'

'You still can. We'll only be upstairs for an hour at the most, and then we can go to Leigh's. Or do the two of you want to be alone?' Joyce said coyly.

'Yes, we do want to be alone, but only because it's not a social visit; it's purely business,' Karen told her. 'Leigh's helping me to learn all about the business because I've decided that from now on I'm going to be spending more time in the office.'

'Why on earth do you want to do that?'

'I need to feel useful. You and Anna look after the house, Leigh and Edith and Grant see to the business, and where do I fit in? Nowhere.'

'Fletcher women don't work,' Joyce said as though it was a mantra. 'They don't need to work. That's what my father and Dan both believed, and that's the way Dan wanted it to be for you, too.'

'Grandfather died long ago, and Dan's not here either,' Karen reminded her aunt, the familiar lump coming into her throat at the thought. 'Things have changed, Joyce. There are no Fletcher men around now to make us sit on silk cushions and sew fine seams.' Then as clouds swept across the sky and a gust of wind skittered across from the shrubbery to whisk about them, she shivered. 'Let's go in; it's getting chilly out here.'

'Who's idea was it to invite us?' she wondered aloud when she and her aunt went into the hall after dinner. 'Grant's, or Belinda's?'

'She didn't say, but it's a nice idea. You know me, darling, I get on well with everyone, but I never know where I am with Belinda. Tonight will give us a chance to get to know her.' She hesitated, then said slowly, 'You must have noticed that she carries quite a torch for Leigh. Not that he's interested.'

Karen raised her eyebrows. 'You've asked him how he feels about Belinda?'

'Of course not, but everyone knows that you're the only woman he cares about.'

'Joyce . . .'

'Right from the moment he first set eyes on you,' her aunt prattled on. 'And I should know, since I was there at the time. And he kept on caring even when you married . . .'

'I miss being able to use this staircase every day,' Karen interrupted as they began to mount the graceful, curving staircase. 'It's so elegant.'

'Isn't it?' Joyce, immediately distracted from what she had been saying, trailed a beringed hand lovingly over the polished banister. 'I remember as if it was yesterday, standing in the hall with Danny, watching my mother coming down from her bedroom, dressed for a dinner party. She looked so regal!'

From what Karen had gathered from her father and Anna, Grandmother Fletcher had been more regal than any royal personage. She had ruled the household, and her son and daughter, with a rod of iron.

'She always wore such rustley clothes,' Joyce chattered on, 'and lily of the valley perfume. Then just as her foot touched the bottom step, Father would come out from his stu . . .'

Her voice trailed away. Following her gaze, Karen saw that Belinda waited for them on the top step, one hand resting lightly on the banister, looking for all the world like the mistress of the house instead of a lodger.

It was strange to be a visitor in what had once been the upstairs floor of the family home and then the flat she had shared with Grant. For the first few moments after entering the lounge – once her grandparents' bedroom – Karen quartered the room with swift glances. Most of the furniture that she and Grant had chosen together was still there, but it had been moved about, and there were little touches – a cluster of photographs featuring the Roberts family, some unfamiliar ornaments, a richly coloured throw rug over the back of the sofa – that showed Belinda's touch.

'How are you?' Grant asked almost at once.

'If you mean, how do I feel about Monty, I'm coping. I spent the day with Charlie, and that helped.'

He grinned. 'I'd say that that was the best thing you could have done. I was wondering . . . is it too soon to offer, or would you like to get another puppy?'

'For goodness' sake, Grant,' Joyce said sharply, then flushed as he and Karen stared at her. 'I mean, of course it's too soon. Give the poor girl time to get over Monty's loss.'

'I agree,' Belinda said smoothly. 'I never cared for dogs, and neither does Joyce, do you?'

'Well, I . . .' Karen's aunt had the grace to look embarrassed. 'I grew quite fond of Monty,' she said awkwardly.

'I know that he was a trial to you at times, Joyce. And thank you for the thought, Grant, but I think I'd like to leave it for a while before I even think of another pet.'

To Karen's surprise it was Belinda who changed the subject, asking Joyce something about her stage career. It was a subject Joyce never tired of; indeed, Dan Fletcher had often wondered aloud how she had managed to make her one short year as an actress stretch into memories that had taken over twenty years in the telling. As she talked and Belinda listened with apparent fascination, Karen drew Grant aside.

'Grant, I'm sorry about rushing off this morning . . .'

'It's understandable. You were very upset.'

She nodded, but said nothing. It helped a little to know that he had misinterpreted her sudden fear of him.

'Actually, I had been about to say, when you dashed off, that I'm sorry about the other afternoon.'

'So that's why we're here,' she said without thinking, then thought, as his eyes darkened, that she had pushed him to the verge of yet another quarrel.

But he settled for, 'Not entirely.'

'I'm sorry too, about the things I said. They were uncalled for.'

'We're like rival gangs in a playground, aren't we? Always sniping at each other.'

'We'll have to stop that, Grant. I'm planning to become more involved in the business, and . . .'

'Edith told me.'

Karen glanced across at the others, still deep in conversation. 'How do you feel about it?'

'It's your company and you have every right to spend more time there. As a matter of fact, that's why I asked Belinda to invite you and Joyce up here. I thought it would give me the chance to tell you a bit more about the new cloth.'

'Good. Go ahead.' Karen tried hard to follow as he talked about costs, production and sales promotions. By the time he stopped talking and poured more coffee for them both she was beginning to share his interest in the new project.

'It sounds feasible, but I don't know enough to be of any use to you . . .'

'I'm going to be frank, Karen. We both know that Leigh would do anything for you, so I'm hoping that you'll agree to talk to him about agreeing to release just one machine for this new job. And don't tell me again that you don't want to take sides; taking sides and making decisions are part of being an active member of the Fletcher board, like it or not.'

'I've realised that. I'll do what I can to help you, Grant. I'm going over to see Leigh when I leave here; I could try speaking to him about your cloth, but I don't know if . . .'

He grinned down at her. 'That's brilliant! There's a single machine on its own in a small workshop; Ramsay reckons that it would be ideal, and I'm sure that if anyone can persuade Leigh to give us a crack at it, it's you!'

Karen had her doubts, but his enthusiasm had caught her interest. If Grant got his chance, and the material turned out to be as good as he anticipated, it would make a good start to her involvement in the business. And if it was a failure, a small voice at the back of her mind whispered, it could be a personal disaster. She tried to push the warning to one side. Her father had had every faith in Grant where the company was concerned, and it was only fair that she give him the opportunity to prove his worth.

'There's Forbes . . .' she ventured.

'Leave him to me; I think I can talk him round. And Edith's all for it.'

'You've become quite friendly, you and Edith.'

He looked surprised. 'She's been very supportive.'

Then Belinda suddenly appeared between them, linking her arm in Grant's and announcing, 'I think that you two have gossiped for long enough.'

A gust of wind eddied round the house and, although the heavy curtains were drawn, Karen heard raindrops rattling against the glass. The bad weather forecast for the night had arrived.

'You certainly seem to have plenty to talk about,' Joyce put in, her eyes bright with interest as she looked from Karen to Grant, and back again.

'Business, sweetheart, just business. I meant to ask you: you didn't see Dan's watch downstairs, did you?'

Joyce frowned. 'No. You haven't lost it, have you?' The watch, an old-fashioned gold hunter with a long chain, had been handed down to Dan Fletcher by his own father, and with no son of his own to pass it to, he had left it to Grant, his son-in-law.

'I can't have lost it,' he said now. 'I took it down to your dinner party, Joyce, to let Edith see it, and I haven't seen it since. When Karen . . .' He stopped, then went on, awkwardly: 'When you took ill, Karen, I must have put it down somewhere. Don't worry, I'll have a proper look for it at the weekend.'

'And I'll check the living room downstairs,' Karen promised. 'It might have slipped down the side of a chair.' She knew how much Grant valued the watch, which he looked on as a good-luck symbol.

'Thanks. Who wants more coffee?'

Karen, mindful of Leigh waiting for her, made her excuses. 'But you stay, Joyce.'

'Why not?' Grant agreed. 'I'm going out myself, but Belinda's here for the evening.'

Joyce opted to leave with Karen, who asked, as they went back down the staircase, 'Well, did you and Belinda get to know each other?'

'She was very nice, but even when I was telling her what she wanted to know about thespian life in London, I got the impression that she wasn't really listening. If you ask me, she had been told to keep me busy so that you and Grant could have a little tête-à-tête.'

'Actually, we had a business discussion. And that is all we'll have, from now on,' Karen added firmly as they arrived in the entrance hall. It was getting dark, but the heavy curtains had not yet been drawn across the windows on either side of the front door.

Joyce began to draw them, then paused to peer out into the night. 'It's pouring now; why don't you phone Leigh and tell him to come over here?'

Karen, knowing that if he did come over, Joyce would only turn the meeting into a social occasion, shook her head. 'He would have to bring a whole lot of papers and files with him. It'll only take me a few minutes to run along the path through the shrubbery. Anyway, I could do with a breath of fresh air.'

To one side of the hall there was a small cloakroom where an assortment of coats, scarves, boots and umbrellas was kept for general use. She wrapped herself in a light-coloured raincoat, tied a scarf about her head and took an umbrella; then, after consideration, she replaced it in the stand. A narrow strip of shrubbery separated the two houses, and a pathway had been beaten through it to save a walk down one drive, along the road and up the other. The umbrella would be of help when she was crossing the lawn, but once she was in the shrubbery it would only be a nuisance. She found a plastic rainhood, and tied it over her head instead. Then she took a small pocket torch from a shelf and slid it into her pocket.

The rain was coming down hard when she opened the door. 'Wait . . .' Joyce followed her on to the top step. 'I'll get a coat and come with you.'

'You'd just get bored listening to the two of us talking business,' Karen argued. 'Go back in before you catch a chill.' And she hurried down the steps before Joyce had time to argue.

Eight

O nce on the gravel drive, she looked back and was relieved to see that the door was closing.

Turning back to the garden, she saw nothing but darkness. She hesitated, blinking rain from her eyes and giving herself time to become accustomed to her surroundings before venturing on to the lawn. As she approached the shrubbery and heard it rustling in the wind, she hesitated and went back to the driveway. The bushes would be soaking; it might be wiser to go the long way round, down her drive and along the road to Leigh's gate. But she had only taken a dozen steps when a trickle of icy rain found its way between the plastic hood and the upturned collar of her coat to snake its way down her neck.

Karen, realising that she would be soaked whichever way she went, spun round and made for the bushes. At least she would reach shelter more quickly this way.

She knew the path so well that she could have run through it with her eyes shut; but now, as she stepped into its dripping, wind-lashed fringes, she wished that she had agreed to let her aunt come with her. But it was too late, and in any case it was time she stopped depending on other people all the time. Although the bushes, pressing in on either side and arching overhead, deflected the worst of the rain, it filtered through to splash on to her face. The wind sighed through the branches, making them creak and groan, and the leaves hushed them timidly but to no avail.

When Karen glanced back, she could glimpse the light outside her own door fitfully between tossing branches, but there was only darkness ahead because a slight bend in the path hid Leigh's house from sight. She switched the torch on and was grateful for the company of its narrow beam. Normally, Monty would have been with her, she thought, pain clutching at her heart. Life was not the same without the little dog's enthusiastic, tail-wagging presence. She wished with all her heart that she could turn the clock back and change the impulse that had sent him off on his own to find and eat the poison that had killed him.

She struggled on, torchlight showing that she was almost at the bend in the path. A few more steps and she would see Leigh's house lights; then she would be clear of the shrubbery and on to his driveway.

Just as she was reassuring herself with this thought, the torch beam picked up something small and pale on the path just ahead of her feet. Karen stopped abruptly, angling the torch downwards to illuminate it properly. Her heart began to hammer as she realised that she was looking at a hand, motionless and white against the dark earth, palm upwards and fingers curled.

For several seconds the dark night seemed to swirl round Karen's head. The torch beam, apparently of its own volition, moved along the hand to a wrist protruding from a light-coloured sleeve. She knelt in the mud and touched the hand. It was warm, but unresponsive. The frail light travelled on up the arm to a shoulder. Karen took hold of it and turned, pulled; something glinted in the light of the torch as the body obediently rolled over and then, as she glimpsed the distorted face and the staring eyes, she screamed and jumped up.

The torch slipped from her nerveless fingers and the light went out, leaving her alone in the moaning darkness except for the huddled body at her feet.

'Oh God, oh God . . .' she panted, diving after the torch, scrabbling in the soft muddy earth, willing the small solid metal shape of it into the palm of her hand; but it was not to be found. At length Karen struggled to her feet and, crushing herself against the bushes so as not to stumble over whoever lay on the path, managed to get past the body.

Then she ran as best she could, crashing through the bushes until she finally burst through the narrow opening that led into Leigh's garden. Although her knees felt like jelly, fear – fear of the still figure she had just left, fear of others who might be hidden among the bushes – gave her the strength to hurl herself forward across the driveway towards the front door.

She hammered frantically on the panels, and when his housekeeper opened the door, she almost fell into the hallway.

'Mrs Roberts! My dear, whatever's happened? Has there been an accident?'

'Where's Leigh? I have to see him!'

'He's working in his study. Sit down, my dear, and I'll fetch him.' The woman tried to ease Karen down on to a chair, but she broke away, stumbling to the study door. From behind its panels came the strains of classical music. The handle refused to move beneath her wet fingers, so she fisted them and banged on the door, calling his name, clutching at him when he finally appeared.

'Karen? For God's sake, what's happened?'

'The shrubbery . . . oh, Leigh, it's . . .'

'There was someone in the shrubbery?'

'Someone's been hurt . . . I almost fell over her . . .'

'Brandy, Margaret.' He almost barked the request to his housekeeper, who ran to obey as he half-carried Karen to a chair. In moments he was holding a glass to her lips and ordering, 'Drink it down.'

She did as she was told, feeling the spirit sting the back of her throat and burn down into her stomach.

'Now . . .' Leigh knelt by the chair, holding her close. '. . . can you tell me what happened?'

Margaret Finlay stood behind him, her face pale. 'I was c-coming through the sh-shrubbery when I almost fell over s-someone lying on the ground,' Karen told them both. 'A woman, I think . . .'

'Did you see anyone else?' Leigh asked sharply. Then, as she shook her head, 'You're certain of that, Karen?'

'Yes.'

'I'd better go and have a look. I'll only be a moment,' he added as she tried to hold him back.

'What if . . . it might be dangerous!'

'Mr Bailie,' Margaret said nervously, '. . . perhaps we should leave it to the police.'

'We have to make certain of the facts before we call them. I'll be all right.' Leigh opened a deep drawer and rummaged inside, then brought out a heavy, long-handled torch. 'This would make a good weapon if necessary.' He switched it on to check the battery's strength and, as the ray of light caught his face, highlighting the planes and hollows, it gave his features an added strength that reminded her painfully of Dan. Suddenly she wanted her father so badly that her eyes filled with tears.

'Stay here, both of you; I'll not be long,' Leigh said, and went from the room.

The housekeeper brought a woollen travel rug from the sofa against one wall and wrapped it about Karen.

'Oh, my dear, you're shivering, and no wonder, out there in the dark and the cold with . . . I'll get the fire up to a good blaze.'

But it wasn't cold that made Karen shiver; it was the memory of the sighing leaves and tossing branches, the mud and the dark and that small white hand, lying so still with the fingers curled like unopened petals.

'Why isn't he back yet? Can you see him?'

'He's scarcely had time to reach the bushes, my dear,' the woman reassured her, going to the window and cupping her hands against the glass. 'I can't see a thing; it's black as pitch out there.'

'Phone for the police!'

'Mr Bailie said for us to wait.'

'What if there was someone out there, hiding in the bushes? What if he's attacked Leigh?'

'Oh, I'm sure he can look after him— Here he comes; I can see the light from his torch!' Margaret Finlay opened the French windows, and in a few moments Leigh was in the room, shaking rain from his dark hair.

'Did you . . . did you see anything?'

His face was ashen. 'You're right, Karen; there is someone out there.'

'Who is it?'

He came to her and took both her hands, holding them tightly. 'I don't know. I just know that whoever it is is dead. I'll have to call the police,' he interrupted as she began to ask questions that she knew he could not answer.

Releasing her hands, he went to the phone on the desk. He began to dial a number and then broke the connection almost immediately, punching out a new set of numbers. 'I'd better call Joyce first, in case she decides to follow you over here,' he said over his shoulder. 'Then I'll— Joyce? It's me. Now don't say anything; just listen. Karen's here with me, and she's in a bit of a state. There's been an accident . . . no, Karen's all right, but someone has been hurt in the garden. I'm going to call the police, Joyce, and I want you to stay there until I come over, do you understand? Don't do anything, don't tell anyone; just wait for me. I'll bring Karen home later, when she's calmed down.'

He broke the connection again. 'Let's hope that that holds her for the time being,' he said briefly, and then he was talking to the local police office.

The police arrived swiftly, splintering the dark night outside with their lights. Mercifully, Leigh was allowed to drive Karen home after she had told them all she knew. As he drove past the shrubbery, busy now with torchlight and movement, Karen turned her head away. She would never again be able to take the short cut from one house to the other.

Neither of them spoke during the short journey to the Fletcher house, where Anna and Joyce, their faces blurred with shock, met them at the door.

'Tomorrow,' Leigh said curtly in answer to their questions.

'We'll talk about it tomorrow. For now, just let Karen get to bed.'

Anna insisted on sleeping on the divan in Karen's room, and Karen, restless, and jumping at every imagined sound or movement, was glad of her presence. She finally fell asleep to a lullaby of morning birdsong, and woke to find that she was alone.

After pulling on a sweater and a pair of corduroy trousers she went to the kitchen, following the sound of voices, and found the room full of people. Grant, Belinda, Joyce and Leigh sat at the table while Anna was busy at the stove. The back door was slightly ajar, letting in a shaft of sunlight. Everything looked normal, and yet nothing would ever be the same again.

Leigh rose and went to her immediately. 'How are you, darling?' He kissed her forehead and led her over to the table, drawing a chair out for her.

'I'm . . .' she stopped. 'Fine' seemed such an empty word in the face of the latest tragedy. 'It really happened, then?'

'Unfortunately, it did,' Grant said, then added, looking round the group, 'And now the police are going to want to talk to us – find out where we all were last night.'

'You don't mean that they would suspect any of us?' Joyce asked, shocked.

'A police investigation is like a jigsaw, Joyce. Every little piece could help. One of us might have seen or heard something that means nothing to us, but something to a police officer.'

'I don't have anything to tell them,' Belinda put in. 'After Joyce and Karen left, I stayed upstairs, watching television.'

'It's all right for you two,' Joyce worried; 'you were together, while I was in the living room on my own with nobody to give me an alibi.'

'We weren't together; Grant went out just after you and Karen left,' Belinda said, and then caught her lower lip between her teeth as all eyes turned to her brother.

'Is that true, Roberts?' Leigh asked. 'You were out last night?'

Grant met his gaze. 'For a little while, to visit a friend. That's how I found out what had happened. When I came back, there were police all over the shrubbery.'

'So they've already questioned you?'

'Only to ask who I was, and where I had been. They said that they would speak to me in the morning, which is why I came down here. We're all going to have to be questioned.'

'I've already been through it with them, last night, after I brought Karen back here. I didn't have much to tell,' Leigh went on. 'I was waiting in my study for Karen to arrive and she burst in looking as though she'd seen a ghost.' He gave her a tired smile. 'I have to admit, my love, that I didn't believe you until I saw her for myself.'

'It was a woman, then? I wasn't sure . . .'

'Karen,' Joyce said quietly, reaching out to take her hand, 'it was Helen.'

'Our Helen? Our maid? But it can't have been!'

'I'm afraid it was,' Leigh said quietly. 'Apparently her father identified her early this morning. I had a suspicion when I first went out there; I went back, after I took you home, and told the police about it.'

'So now I'm going to have policemen tramping all over the house, and no help coming in. Not that Helen was all that helpful,' Anna said vehemently, so vehemently that it was clear her anger was a defence against a show of emotion.

'Someone we actually knew – someone who was in this very house – murdered! That's dreadful . . . dreadful!' Joyce dabbed at her eyes with a lacy handkerchief. 'What happened? How did she get there?'

'If I knew that, Miss Joyce, we'd not need the police at all and I'd be making a fortune on the telly like that Miss Marple instead of spending all my days cooking and cleaning and worrying about how I'm going to manage without a woman to do the heavy work.'

'I'll help . . . we'll advertise for another maid . . .'

Anna sniffed. 'I doubt if you'll get any offers, not if they think they might be found dead in the shrubbery.'

'What did you mean, Karen, when you said that it couldn't be Helen?' Belinda asked sharply. Then, as Karen stared at her, almost paralysed with the shock of sudden realisation, 'Who did you expect it to be?'

Karen had to try twice before she found her voice. 'I had meant that it couldn't be someone we know,' she said at last, shakily. 'Then I realised the truth: it wasn't Helen he meant to kill . . . it was me!'

There was silence for a moment, then Belinda said flatly, 'That's nonsense, utter nonsense! Your imagination's working overtime again.'

'But don't you see? Last night, Helen was wearing a light-coloured raincoat. So was I. She was about my height and build, and she has . . . had . . . dark hair in much the same style as mine. The person who killed her thought that it was me, not her!'

'But why would anyone want to harm you, Karen?' Leigh asked patiently, gently. She whirled on him.

'That's what I don't know: why would anyone want to kill me?'

'There you are, then.' Joyce was clearly nervous. She fidgeted with the coffee pot, and went so far as to ask tentatively, 'More coffee, anyone? Karen? You've not had any break . . .'

'But look at what happened at the cottage. Then there was that night in my bedroom . . . and then last night!' Still they stared at her. Karen slammed her fist on the table in sheer frustration. 'Why can't any of you see it? Why won't you help me to work this out?'

'I would, if you could show me proof,' Grant said. 'But at the moment I can't think of any.'

'What sort of proof do you need?' she almost shouted at him. 'My dead body? Would that satisfy you?'

'Now you're just being hysteric—' he began; then, as the

doorbell rang, startling them all, 'That will be the police. Better let them in, Anna.'

'I wouldn't advise it,' an amiable voice said from the back door. 'It'll be the newspaper people. I'm the police. Inspector Sam Crombie.'

Nine

Inspector Crombie came into the kitchen, smiling apologetically at the startled faces around the table. 'Sorry about the sudden appearance; I was just having a general look around, and then I realised from the voices that the people I wanted to speak to were probably quite near.'

He must have heard every word, Karen thought, looking round at the others. Joyce, close to tears, still toyed with the coffee pot while Belinda and Grant, sitting side by side, were carefully expressionless.

'To be honest,' Crombie said, 'the smell of good coffee attracted me too.'

'Would you like some?' Joyce clutched at the offered straw.

'I certainly would. May I?' he asked; when she nodded, he pulled out a chair and lowered his gangling length on to it, beaming as he accepted the steaming cup, and sniffing the aroma before taking his first sip.

'Nectar . . . thank you!' He divided his smile between Joyce and Anna. 'Now then . . .' He pulled a notebook from his pocket and opened it. 'If you wouldn't mind identifying yourselves . . .' As he named them, they each raised a hand, reverting to classroom habits. It would have been funny, Karen thought bleakly, if it wasn't such a tragedy. 'Mr Bailie, Miss Fletcher and Miss Harper, Mr Roberts . . . and Mrs Roberts?' He raised an eyebrow at Belinda.

'Mrs Solomon,' she snapped. 'This is my brother and that –' with a jerk of the head towards Karen '– is Mrs Roberts.'

75

'Ah.' Crombie looked from Grant to Karen, his eyes measuring the space between them and then taking in Leigh, still standing behind Karen, his hands on her shoulders. Then he glanced at Joyce as she said pleadingly, 'It was an accident, surely, Inspector. Helen must have tripped over a tree root, hit her head on a stone in the dark . . . ?'

'We don't know a lot at this early stage, madam, but we do know that the young lady was done to death,' he said gently. 'Murdered. And since it happened quite a distance from the road, and she was known to you, I doubt if it was a casual, unpremeditated murder.'

Leigh's fingers tightened on Karen's shoulders as though in warning, but it was too late. 'It wasn't unpremeditated!' The words were out before she knew it, and Crombie's interested gaze returned to her.

'You have some additional information, Mrs Roberts?'

'I think the murder was deliberate, but I don't think that whoever it was meant to kill Helen. It should have been me.' Now that she had the floor, Karen found it hard to sound convincing.

'You, Mrs Roberts? You don't strike me as the type of person to be singled out for murder.'

'Of course she isn't; she's overwrought, that's all. She hasn't got over a nasty accident she had a few weeks ago . . .' Joyce's voice had begun to shake a little and Grant leaned over to put his hand on hers.

'It's all right, Joyce; don't get upset.'

'Accident?' Crombie probed.

'At our . . . at my wife's country cottage,' Grant explained. 'She was attacked by an intruder while she was there alone. She only came out of hospital about two weeks ago.'

The detective looked at Karen with renewed interest. 'Of course. I knew of it, though I wasn't on the case myself. They haven't got anyone yet, have they?'

'Not yet. My wife doesn't believe that she disturbed a thief who panicked. She thinks that someone deliberately tried to kill her.'

'And failed, so he tried again last night – is that it, Mrs Roberts?'

'It could be. You see, Helen wore a light raincoat, didn't she? I remember seeing her arm in the light from the torch . . .' Karen's voice faltered at the recollection, but she made herself go on. 'I wore one very like it. We keep a selection of old coats in the cloakroom by the door for when anyone goes out into the garden or across to see Leigh – Mr Bailie. There were two light-coloured coats there. They both belonged to me.

'Do you use that path through the shrubbery quite often?'

'We all do.'

'Does "all" include your maid?'

'As far as I know she had little occasion to use that path, but she might have. She could easily have been mistaken for me in the dark.'

'Who might have known that you would use that path last night?'

She hadn't had time to think of that. 'Well . . . Leigh, of course, because we'd made arrangements the other day, though I was later than planned because of having coffee with Grant and Belinda first. And Joyce knew.'

'And I knew because you told me that you were going over to see Leigh,' Grant broke in. 'But I didn't try to kill you.'

She felt her face colour at the dry tone in his voice. 'I didn't imply that . . .'

'You've just said that the only people who knew you were using that path last night were the people round this table.' He released Joyce's hand and stood up. 'Do you seriously think that one of us is out to harm you . . . to kill you?'

'I don't know what to think!'

'Perhaps it's time to get this investigation on a more formal footing.' Sam Crombie pushed himself back from the table. 'I wonder if I could get the use of a room in this house for the time being?'

'Of course. The dining room?' Karen looked at Anna, who sighed audibly, then nodded.

'Thank you, madam. I'll tell my sergeant to present himself

at the front door, and if those of you who have business to see to could just let him know where you can be contacted during the day, I'll not detain you any longer.'

'This must be a very nasty shock to all of you,' the Inspector said sympathetically when he had returned to the kitchen.

'I feel as if I'm in the middle of a nightmare,' Joyce said pathetically.

'I can understand that. That's the way mur— sudden death takes most people. Now, madam, I would like to have a word with your niece first. That should give you some time to rest quietly.'

He opened the door for Karen and made sure that she was comfortably seated in the dining room before asking his first question. Although he had a youthful face, with wide, clear grey eyes and a long mouth, Karen realised, when she looked at him more closely and noticed the thick, dark hair greying at the temples, that he was older than she had first thought. His manner was quiet, sympathetic, almost self-effacing, and she was in the middle of describing how she had found the body lying across her path the previous night before she glanced over at the young sergeant sitting unobtrusively in a corner, scribbling in a notebook, and realised that the interrogation had begun.

Crombie listened without interruption, his face lighting up when Anna brought in a tray of fresh coffee. Taking his cup, he settled himself into a comfortable chair. 'If you wouldn't mind staying for a moment or two?' he asked Anna; then, to Karen, 'I'm sorry, Mrs Roberts. You were saying . . . ?'

'I haven't really got anything more to tell you. I touched her hand and it was still warm, but she wasn't . . . she didn't respond.' She swallowed hard, then made herself go on. 'I managed to step round her and then I ran next door. Leigh – Mr Bailie – was in his study and he left me with his housekeeper while he went out to the shrubbery. Then he came back and phoned you.'

'You didn't call the police while you and the housekeeper were waiting in the study, to save time?'

She shook her head. 'I couldn't think straight, and Leigh said to do nothing until he had made sure that I really had seen someone – Helen – lying there.'

'He doubted your word?'

She felt colour come into her cheeks. 'It was an unlikely situation, and with the wind and the rain, I suppose he wondered if I had made a mistake,' she said levelly; then, 'I may have come over as an hysterical idiot in the kitchen, Inspector, but I can assure you that I am not a fool.'

'I never for a moment thought that, Mrs Roberts.' His voice was so gentle, his expression so serene, that she believed him.

'I suppose – waiting in the study for Leigh to come back – that I was hoping that I *had* imagined it.'

'But sadly, you hadn't. Do you recognise this?' Crombie pushed a plastic envelope towards her.

'It's my torch . . . I dropped it when I saw Helen. I couldn't find it again.' A sudden picture flashed into Karen's mind: the dark path, sighing trees, herself scrambling around, trying to locate the torch; her fingers brushing against the dead hand . . .

He nodded and put the envelope aside. 'So you and Mr Bailie's housekeeper waited until Mr Bailie came back and confirmed that you really had seen the unfortunate girl. And then he phoned the local police.'

'Yes . . . no.' Karen suddenly remembered. 'Not immediately. He called my aunt first.' Then, when he raised an eyebrow: 'He was worried in case she decided to follow me. He didn't want her to see . . .'

'Quite.' Crombie turned to Anna, who had ignored his gesture towards a chair and remained standing, her hands clasped tightly before her. 'When did you last see Helen Watson, Miss Harper?'

'After dinner last night. We had something to eat in the kitchen; then she did the washing-up while I got on with some baking for today. I'd told her that I wanted her to stay behind to help me to clean out the larder. She was supposed to do it earlier, but she'd arrived late and not bothered. When I looked up, she was gone without as much as a word of explanation.' Anna's mouth tightened. 'She was good at slipping away; we'd had words about it before. She was always in a hurry to meet one boyfriend or another.'

'Do you know the latest boyfriend's name?'

'There was more than one, and I could never keep up with the names. She was a flighty girl.'

Crombie nodded and said mildly, 'I'll follow that up. Now, why would she be on that path?'

'She may have been taking a short cut through Mr Bailie's garden to the road,' Karen volunteered. 'It's quicker than going down our own drive.'

'Or she could have arranged to meet someone there. The trees make a good shelter,' Anna put in.

'Did she usually leave at around the same time?'

'She was supposed to work on until everything was done and I told her she could go, but she was always itching to get away as soon as dinner was served. She has . . . had,' Anna corrected herself, her voice suddenly harsh, '. . . a poor sense of responsibility.'

'What . . . what exactly happened to her?' Karen asked unwillingly. She wanted to forget, yet some part of her mind needed to face up to the full horror of the girl's death.

'We're still waiting for the post-mortem results, but it seems fairly obvious that she was strangled . . . with a cord or something like that. She probably didn't know a thing,' the detective added consolingly. 'It must have been very quick. Can I ask exactly who lives in this house? I understand, Mrs Roberts, that you and your husband are living apart?'

'Yes, but since he's the office manager at the family business it suits him to go on living in the flat upstairs. His sister moved in with him not long after we came to that arrangement.'

'You mentioned earlier that you and your aunt spent some time upstairs last night. Do you all move freely between both floors?'

'We respect each other's privacy,' Karen said carefully.

'There's a side door to the flat, and Grant and Belinda use that most of the time. If they're coming down here, or we've been invited upstairs, then we use the inner staircase from the hall.'

'But you're still on friendly terms. For instance, you were all together in the kitchen this morning.'

'Yes, we are on good terms.'

'Mr Roberts phoned first thing this morning about what had happened,' Anna broke in, 'and so did Mr Bailie, so I asked them both to come over. I knew you'd want to meet all of us as soon as possible.'

'Very wise, Miss Harper,' Crombie said approvingly, and she simpered slightly.

'I read crime novels in my spare time,' she admitted, 'and I never miss programmes like "The Bill" on television, so I have an idea of the way things are done.'

'You never cease to surprise me, Anna,' Karen said when they had been dismissed and Joyce sent for. 'I didn't know that you were an amateur criminologist.'

'We all have our private pleasures,' the housekeeper told her primly, 'but we don't have to inflict them on others. Now then, I could do with a hand in the kitchen, since I don't have Helen any more.'

Joyce joined them a quarter of an hour later, pink-cheeked and fussed.

'I didn't know what to say!'

'All you needed to do was answer the questions,' Anna said drily.

'I gathered from what the inspector said that you called poor Helen a flirt, and said that she was lazy, Anna. You shouldn't speak ill of the dead!' Joyce protested.

'I speak as I find and the man needs to know the truth, Miss Joyce; it's the only way he can find out what happened. They can't catch the murderer if they don't know anything about the victim. You', Anna pointed out, 'scarcely knew the girl.'

'You're right.' Karen felt guilty. A young woman in her employment, someone she had seen at least once every day for the past four months or so, had been murdered on her property, and yet she had known nothing about her.

'I was always kind to her, and she seemed civil enough to me.' Joyce fished a small handkerchief from her pocket and dabbed at her eyes. 'That poor young girl, struck down like a flower in full bloom!'

'She never looked very blooming to me,' Anna said drily as she loaded the dishwasher.

Ten

'I would have called you as soon as I heard' – Charlie's voice rushed down the wires and into the telephone receiver like a breath of fresh air – 'but Forbes said to leave it over the weekend at least. Oh lovey, what a terrible thing to happen! Is there anything I can do?'

'Short of turning the clock back, there's nothing any of us can do.'

'Do you want me to come over?'

'Can I come to you instead? I'd love to get out of this place for an hour or two.'

'Of course you can, if you're allowed.'

'I've not been charged with murder yet, Charlie.'

'Well I don't know how these police investigations work. I thought you might not be allowed to speak to anyone.'

'That's the jury, in a trial,' Karen explained. 'I'm on my way.'

Half an hour later she burst in through Charlie's door and hugged her friend. 'You have no idea how wonderful it is to get out of that house and away from the atmosphere!'

'Come into the kitchen and tell me about it while I make some coffee,' Charlie ordered; and then, when she had heard the story, 'It's hard to take in. Murder's something that happens somewhere else, to people you've never met. But right here . . .' she shivered and then said soberly, 'I didn't know that poor girl, but just the fact that we lived in the same small town makes it so real, so close!'

'I know.'

83

'Forbes says that the atmosphere at the factory's tense. What's it like at your house?'

'Grim. Joyce keeps getting tearful, and Anna's complaining about having to do everything herself. You'd think that Helen got herself killed just to escape housework. It's Anna's way of coping. I think Helen's death has hit her hard. And I haven't made matters any easier,' Karen admitted wryly, 'turning into a harpy and accusing all and sundry of trying to kill me.'

'What? You're not serious!'

'Charlie, it's happened before, at the cottage and then the night of the party, when someone tried to smother me.'

'Karen, what are you talking about? No, wait,' Charlie commanded as Karen opened her mouth to speak; 'to hang with coffee. I'm going to fetch a good stiff drink for the two of us before you say another word. I think we both need it.'

Karen had thought that it would be hard to go over the story again, but the fact that Charlie, like Sam Crombie, was a sympathetic listener made it easy. 'Now tell me that I'm mad and it's all nonsense . . . please!' she finished with a feeble attempt at humour. Then she realised that it was true. All she really wanted was to be proved wrong. Only then could she let go and start rebuilding her life.

Charlie was sitting, lotus-fashion, on the floor, chain-smoking as she listened. She always smoked in abrupt puffs that belied her casual air.

'You mean you've been carrying those fears around in your head? Oh, Karen, why didn't you tell me this sooner?'

'It's not easy to come out and say that you think your life's in danger.'

'Let's think this thing through. It must have been a burglar that you surprised at the cottage. He hit you for two reasons, the first being that he didn't want you to be able to identify him later, the second that he had to buy time to get away. Why would he then seek you out here, where you're surrounded by friends?'

'What if it wasn't a burglar? What if it was someone I know, someone who had some reason to want to hurt me, or kill me?

The night someone came into my room, Charlie, I had taken a strange turn at the party because I heard something – a voice, a laugh, I don't know exactly. But whatever it was, it terrified me. It took me right back to that time at the cottage. And I told them that. Don't you see? I told whoever it was that I had remembered something. Then I told them that Monty had been in the cottage with me and yet, as far as we know, he didn't try to defend me. Which points to the attacker being someone he knew. Heaven help me, I told them all of that, and a few hours later someone tried to put a pillow over my face.'

'But . . . who would want to harm you?'

'You, for a start.'

Charlie choked on her cigarette. 'Me?' she finally managed to blurt out between coughs.

'Remember the other day, when you said you'd hated me that summer when Forbes was keen on me?'

Charlie gave a final cough then stubbed the cigarette out in an ashtray. 'That does it; this time I'm really going to give these things up! You idiot, I was talking about years ago. You don't seriously think that I want to kill you? Or that I ever did?'

'No, but the point is, Charlie, that at the time I had no idea how you felt about me. I was so wrapped up in myself that I didn't even notice you were hurting. How many other people have I upset or wounded without realising it?'

'None, honestly. If it was me, I could understand it: people who bought my pictures or designs then went crazy after days and weeks of living with them and decided to murder the creator . . . but you? Forget it, Karen.'

But Karen couldn't give up that easily. 'What about Joyce?'

'Motive?'

'My father went to London and found her, then made her come back home after she had escaped her parents to make her way as an actress . . .'

'He didn't make her return. My mother told me once that when your father found Joyce she was out of work and finding it hard to make ends meet, so returning to a comfortable home was probably a relief to her. She just doesn't want to admit it. And why would she take it out on you anyway? If she had really been miffed at having her career brought to a sudden end, she could have stuck a bread knife in your father years ago.' Then, when Karen chuckled at the thought of gentle, diminutive Joyce Fletcher attacking her burly, domineering brother: 'You see? You can't imagine her doing anything more violent than spraying the roses for greenfly, can you? Count Joyce out.'

'Leigh?'

'Now you're just being silly. He wears his heart on his sleeve as far as you're concerned.'

'I said I would marry him and then I opted for Grant. That would make anyone bitter.'

'Leigh's not the sort of man to bear grudges. In any case, he's back in the running now that you and Grant have split up.'

'Or so everyone seems to assume.'

'You'd be crazy not to marry him, Karen. He's just what you need in a husband.'

'That's what I thought about Grant,' Karen said wryly. 'Charlie, I can't make a second mistake. What was it that Lady Whatsit said in *The Importance of Being Earnest*? Once is unfortunate, but twice is carelessness?'

'Something like that. I'm sure it will happen, in time, and it won't become careless. As for Grant, being married to you or not being married to you doesn't affect his place in the firm, so you surely don't have him on your list of enemies. So that leaves Belinda. She's a dark horse, isn't she? I can't take to her at all, though she's got lovely bone structure. If only I liked her, I could ask her to sit for me.'

'She certainly dislikes me and she makes no secret of it, but I can't see her killing in cold blood,' Karen said thoughtfully. 'She's more the deep, passionate type, if you ask me.'

'I know what you mean; I've noticed her about town now and again with Leigh. She might want you out of the way, so that she can get a clear shot at him,' Charlie said thoughtfully.

'She doesn't like animals. She might have put down the poison that killed Monty . . .'

'Whoa!' Charlie held up a warning hand. 'Don't let's get carried away, girl; I was only joking. You're in danger of talking yourself into believing anything, and that's dangerous. Do you have any proof that Belinda poisoned Monty?'

'Grant bought him for me, as a wedding present. She's very possessive where Grant's concerned, have you noticed?'

'I'd noticed that she seemed to resent you and her brother being so happy together; but now that you're apart why should she care enough to hurt you, or Monty?'

'It could be someone employed by the company, someone who had a grudge against my father. He was very outspoken at times.'

'And it could be Dr Jekyll or Mr Hyde, but my money's on Jack the Ripper. If anything happened to you, what would become of Fletcher and Company?' Charlie wanted to know.

'If I don't leave any children to inherit, then everything goes to Joyce.'

'Who would sell out because I'm sure she would have no interest in keeping the place going. And then all your employees, including Forbes, Leigh, Grant and Edith would have to look for other jobs. So why would any of them want to kill the woman who pays their salaries? You were supposed to come here to get your mind off murder.' Charlie got to her feet. 'Come back to the kitchen with me. I'm plagued by this uneasy suspicion that if I don't have food waiting for the kids after school they'll start eating me.'

'I'd love to see them both, but I'd better go. I want to look in at the factory on my way home.'

'Come again soon, and phone any time you want a chat. But promise me one thing, Karen: don't start getting paranoid about this business,' Charlie cautioned anxiously.

As Karen left her car and crossed to the office entrance she met Grant on his way out. His eyes searched her face. 'No news?'

'Nothing.'

'How are you?'

'Coping, though I'm beginning to feel that I'd like to resign from the human race.'

'I can't say I blame you. It's been rough for you, one way or another. By the way, I don't suppose you've found Dan's fob watch?'

She had forgotten about the watch. 'Not as far as I know.'

'I'll never forgive myself if it has really gone missing.'

'It doesn't matter, Grant; it's only a possession.' She had meant to offer consolation, but his lips tightened before he said sharply, 'It was Dan's and he entrusted it to me. I'll find it!' Then, as she said nothing: 'Have you had a word with Leigh about . . . ?'

'How could I, with all that's been going on?'

His eyebrows tucked together in a familiar frown. 'I know that this is a bad time for you, Karen, but this project won't wait for much longer. Mike Ramsay's just told me that another company's showing interest in him.'

'Then perhaps you should just let him go. I doubt if Leigh would listen to me anyway. I've got to prove that I'm worth listening to and my track record to date hasn't been good.'

'But . . . oh, forget it,' Grant snapped. 'If Leigh and Forbes can't look ahead, it's their loss!'

She laid a hand on his arm as he began to push past her. 'Grant, you won't do anything foolish, will you?'

'Foolish? You mean, like walking out? That might be for the best . . . all round.'

'Don't do that, and don't pick a fight with Leigh over this project of yours. We need to win his co-operation.'

'We?'

'I'll try, but it might take a week or two. Can you get Mike Ramsay to hold back on that other firm?'

He hesitated, then said, 'I'll tell him that things are moving. Try for sooner rather than later, will you?'

'I'll do my best.'

The tension between them began to ease. 'Good girl; I knew

you wouldn't let me down.' The beginnings of a smile began to soften his mouth.

'I haven't achieved anything yet.'

'But you can do it. Just remember that you're Dan Fletcher's daughter,' he said; then, 'I wish he was still here. I could use his help right now.'

'So could I,' Karen said from the heart.

She found Edith working in her office.

'Perfect timing: I was just going to have some coffee. You'll join me?' she asked, crossing to the percolator that was kept in constant readiness.

Handing a cup to Karen, she leaned back against her desk, crossing her shapely legs at the ankle. 'You look well in spite of everything that's been happening.'

'Bless you for saying that instead of asking how I am.'

'I heard that you had been to the cottage. Good idea.'

'Forbes and Charlie are going there next month for a holiday. It gave me the perfect chance to check the place out – you know, flush out ghosts and lay them to rest.'

'Did you find any?'

'Not one. Though I did find one thing . . .' Karen paused as the assistant came in and went out, and when they were alone again she asked, 'What do you know about the name Jopling?'

'Jopling and Ferguson – that's the name of the firm that was interested in buying us out. Why do you— Here you are.' She whipped a tissue from the box on her desk and held it out. 'Put that under your cup; it'll mop up the spilled coffee. It didn't go on to your skirt, did it?'

'Never mind the coffee' – Karen waved the tissue away – 'what did you say about a buyout?'

'You didn't remember? But you knew Jopling's name.'

'I found it on a torn scrap of paper in the cottage, and for some reason it seemed familiar. But . . . a buyout?' Karen said in disbelief.

'Oh dear! Karen, it's over and done with. We – the board

– couldn't make any decisions while you were in hospital, and Jopling and Ferguson pulled out and found another firm suited to a takeover.'

'Just as well, since I wouldn't have wanted to lose the family firm,' Karen said; then, as Edith hesitated, chewing at her lower lip, 'There's more to it than that, isn't there?'

'It's over, Karen, and you've just said that you're happy with the result . . .'

'There's more. Tell me, Edith!'

Edith was standing by the window now; the sun glinted on her silver hair and silhouetted her neat figure. 'The thing is, my dear, that the last time I saw you before the accident at the cottage, you were talking about accepting the offer. If you hadn't been in hospital – if you hadn't had that accident – you might well have outvoted the rest of us and let Fletcher and Company go.'

Karen stared at Edith, unable to believe her ears. Then she said shakily, 'Why would I want to sell the business?'

'It was a difficult time for you. You'd been restless and unhappy ever since you and Grant broke up. You weren't interested in the company – and we're all delighted that you want to become more involved now,' Edith added swiftly. 'Dan would have been pleased.'

Karen shook her head. 'Don't change the subject. Tell me more about this offer.'

Edith shrugged helplessly then said, 'The day before your accident you told me that you were seriously considering pushing your divorce through quickly, selling up and leaving the area. I tried to talk you out of it but . . . you can be a determined person, Karen.'

'"Stubborn" is a better word, or perhaps "wilful". I'm beginning to dislike the sort of person I was before I got that bang on the head.'

'If it's any consolation, you've changed quite a bit since then. My dear,' Edith said gently, 'you were quite moody and withdrawn after you and Grant split up, but that's all over now, and it's so good to know that you care more about the firm.'

She cast a glance at the closed door and then said, her voice lowered, 'Grant's told me that you've agreed to support him and Mike Ramsay.'

'Has he?'

'Yes. I think you're doing the right thing there. Dan would have been interested in this new idea, and these days I see more of him in you now than ever before.'

'Perhaps I should be grateful to that burglar for banging some sense into my head,' Karen suggested wryly.

'I wouldn't go as far as that. You always were Dan's daughter, my dear. You only needed to mature a little.'

'How can you have put up with me for so long? You've always been a special part of my life, Edith.' Karen pressed on when the older woman flushed: 'You always had time for me when my father brought me to the office, and when I was a teenager and I needed someone to talk to, I came to you, remember? You've been like an older sister and a mother all rolled into . . .' Karen stopped short as something suddenly occurred to her. Something that she should have thought of a long time ago.

'Don't be silly,' Edith admonished her briskly. 'It was my pleasure. After all, I didn't have a family of my own.'

'No, you didn't. Not even a boyfriend, as far as I know. You were always here, for me and my father, and I never ever wondered about that.'

'We can't all meet Mr Right. Besides, I'm a career girl; I always was.'

'Married to Fletcher and Company. How could machinery and offices take the place of a husband, Edith? Or was everything you wanted right here?' Karen asked, a thought beginning to form. 'Here . . . in this building?'

Eleven

'Y̶ou have changed, haven't you?' Edith asked after a long silence. 'You never used to be so aware of what was happening to other people. As you so shrewdly put it, my dear, everything I wanted was right here, with Dan.'

'You . . . and my father . . . ?'

'It's history now, and Dan's gone, so there isn't any point in my denying it any more. Not to you.'

'Did he know?'

'Oh yes, it was mutual. Did you never guess? I sometimes thought that you might, as you grew older.'

'Not once.' More proof, Karen thought, that she had been too absorbed in herself to notice what was happening to the people she was supposed to love. 'Did anyone else know about it?'

Edith gave her a wry smile. 'We didn't announce our feelings, or parade them around openly. But I think that Grant and Leigh must both have realised, because after Dan died they were both especially kind to me. It's difficult, you see, to be a mistress at a time like that. I had no right to mourn with you, or to be comforted, though I was just as devastated as you and Joyce.'

'Joyce . . . ?'

'If she knew, or suspected, about me and her brother, she said nothing to me about it.'

'But why didn't the two of you get married? You were both free to do as you wanted.'

Edith's hand was steady as she lit a cigarette. 'Karen, I loved Dan Fletcher with all my heart, and I'll go on loving him until the end of my life. He owned me, perhaps because he made me what I am today.' She smiled, her face softened by memories. 'When I came to this company straight from secretarial school I was a gawky, shy eighteen-year-old without any faith in myself whatsoever . . .'

Eighteen. Karen's mind flashed back over ten years to her own memories of being eighteen years old. She had been so confident then, so sure that life owed her nothing but good things, and that she had some special right to them. A lot had changed in the past ten years: she had started a painful learning process, and it had a long way still to go.

'About a year after I started,' Edith was saying, 'your grandfather died and Dan took over Fletcher's. He needed a secretary and for some reason he chose me. He must have seen something in me that nobody else saw, including me. He was so patient, Karen, so kind. He taught me the business from the inside out and he trained me to work with him rather than for him. He did the same for Leigh and Grant when they came on to the staff. He gave me the confidence to make the most of myself. I fell in love with him almost at once, and eventually a miracle happened: he fell in love with me too. But marriage was never an option because Dan knew that, to my mind, marriage would have included children. And he felt that you might resent anyone else coming into the life you shared with him. He loved you too much to let that happen. He was very honest about it. He gave me the chance to break away and find someone else, someone who wanted open commitment and children. But for me, it was Dan Fletcher or nobody.'

'All these years you worked alongside him to build up his business, and you didn't get anything back.'

'Karen,' Edith said gently, 'if you really love someone, then you want whatever they want, no matter what it is.'

'Why didn't you hate me for standing in the way of marriage, and your own family?'

Edith blew a perfectly formed smoke ring then said, 'I think I was quite jealous of you in the early days, which was ridiculous, since you were only a little girl. Then I began

93

to realise that Dan Fletcher's heart was big enough to hold us both, in different ways.'

'And now? Don't you despise me now for what you've lost?'

'Don't be melodramatic, my dear. Why should I blame you for decisions I took? Besides, I have no regrets, only happy memories. That's why I want to stay in this office, to have Dan's daughter as my friend. You keep him alive for me.' She studied the glowing tip of her cigarette then asked, 'Could we change the subject? I find it somewhat embarrassing, discussing my dead lover with his daughter.'

Karen ran her fingers through her hair. 'Yes, of course.' She squared her shoulders and smiled at the older woman, the woman who could, and should, have been her stepmother. 'Would you give Leigh a ring to find out if I can see him for ten minutes before I leave? I promised Grant that I would try to get him to agree to this new business.'

Leigh was tied up for the rest of the morning. 'But he says he'll come over to the house in an hour or so, if that's all right.' Edith raised her eyebrows, and when Karen nodded, she said into the receiver, 'That's fine; she'll see you there.'

Then, putting the phone down: 'Good luck, Karen; I hope you win this one.'

Why had she announced to Edith that she wanted to speed up the divorce and get away from the area? Karen wondered as she drove home. Could she have discovered something about Grant, something so terrible that it had made her want to end the marriage and get away as fast as she could?

Edith's words came back to her. 'I loved Dan, and if you really love someone, then you want whatever they want, no matter what it is.'

That had never applied to her marriage. She and Grant had gone from supreme happiness to bickering, and then to serious quarrels – she remembered that vividly – quarrels they had both been determined to win. Spoiled by her father, Karen had assumed that what suited her would suit Grant, while his stubbornness made him resist her at every turn. It was that same stubbornness that had got him where he was in the business, she thought as she turned off the road and in at the gates – the stubbornness that her father had recognised and liked, possibly because he himself shared it . . . and had passed it down to Karen herself.

Sam Crombie emerged from the shrubbery path as she drove by. She hurried back round the house when she had parked the car and found him still there, staring across the lawn and flowerbeds.

'Do you have any news?'

'Nothing concrete as yet. He smiled at her. I'm afraid you'll have to put up with me for a few days yet, Mrs Roberts. But we hope that it won't be for long.' Then: 'I wonder . . . gardens happen to be a hobby of mine,' he blurted out as though confessing to a minor crime, 'other people's, that is; I never seem to find the time to tend my own. D'you think you could show me round, if you have a minute, that is?'

'Of course, but there's very little garden, as such,' Karen explained as she and the policeman stepped on to the lawn. 'I believe that in my grandfather's time there were more flower beds and a proper kitchen garden, but my father had most of it turned into lawns, and planted the shrubberies all round the perimeter, for privacy. He wasn't very interested in gardens.'

'You still have some handsome flower beds around the lawn, though.'

'Thanks to my green-fingered aunt, and a man who comes in three days a week. I used to love it here,' Karen said as they approached the thick belt of trees and bushes. 'It hides the house from the road, and it made a wonderful play area when I was young.'

'I can believe that.' He stopped at the edge of the lawn and listened for a moment. 'You wouldn't know that the road was there at all.' Then, as they stepped into the shelter of the trees: 'Do you remember seeing your maid wearing a pendant or a locket at any time, Mrs Roberts? Or possibly even a medallion on a fairly hefty chain . . . a token from a boyfriend, say?'

Karen tried to picture the maid as she had seen her about the house. 'I'm ashamed to admit that I never really noticed what Helen wore.'

'That's not surprising; your aunt and your housekeeper both said that. We tend to take other people for granted. I know that when I meet someone I see every day – the woman who sells me a newspaper every morning, for instance – out in the street, away from her usual surroundings, I know that the face is familiar, but I can't place it.' He held back a low tree branch to let her pass and then continued as he followed her: 'If you'd realised you were going to be asked these questions you'd have taken notice. But we never know what lies ahead.'

Nor did Helen, Karen thought, a chill creeping down her spine. Aloud, she asked, 'Is it important? Does that mean that you think the motive was theft?'

'Unfortunately, it doesn't seem so. I asked because we now think that whoever killed her used a chain of some sort. Possibly part of a necklace, but she wasn't wearing anything like that when she was found – oh my word, that's a surprise,' the policeman said as they stepped from a wall of rhododendron bushes and found themselves in a clearing. A circular summer house stood in the middle.

'Well hidden, isn't it? It didn't used to be so overgrown, of course. In my grandfather's time the summer house could be seen from the terrace. This is where I used to hold my dolls' tea parties. I'm afraid it's been neglected,' Karen added apologetically as they went inside. There was still some garden furniture, but it looked dilapidated and sad. 'I don't think anyone's been here since the final tea party.'

'I would have given my eye teeth for a hideaway like this when I was a lad.' Crombie stood in the middle of the room, revolving slowly. 'I wouldn't mind one like it nowadays, where I could smoke my pipe and read my paper of a Sunday afternoon.'

'I should probably renovate it. In fact,' Karen said decisively, seeing the summer house anew through his eyes, 'I will, as soon as the better weather comes al—' She stopped, stared at him, then said, 'I've just remembered something.'

'Yes?'

Karen's knees had started to tremble and she was not sure if her voice would work; she brushed some leaves from the room's wooden bench in order to give herself time to calm a little, then sat down. 'When I found Helen her hand was warm and I thought that she had just fainted, or tripped and banged her head. So I turned her over on to her back. I still had the torch then, and I think I saw something shining –' she put a hand to her own throat '– about here. Then I saw her face and I dropped the torch and . . .'

'Take a few deep breaths, Mrs Roberts,' Crombie advised, his voice calm. 'Put your head . . .'

'I'm all right, I'm not going to faint. It could have been a chain that I saw. You didn't find anything like that?'

'No, we—'

'Karen?' Someone was coming through the shrubbery towards them.

'We're here, Leigh. I've been showing Inspector Crombie round the grounds,' she said as he came into the summer house.

He sat beside her and took her hands. 'You look pale. Have you been badgering her?' he asked the policeman angrily.

'We were just talking, and then I remembered seeing something.'

'Mrs Roberts recalled seeing some sort of chain round her maid's neck that night in the shrubbery,' Crombie said calmly. 'You were the next person to see the bo— the young woman, Mr Bailie. Did you see any sign of it?'

'No, but I wasn't looking for clues. I just wanted to make sure of the facts before calling you people. Is it important?'

'We think her killer may have used a strong chain, larger than that normally worn by women. Something with a medallion on it rather than a locket or a jewel.'

Leigh put an arm about Karen, and she leaned gratefully against his shoulder.

'If something the girl was wearing was used to kill her,' he said over her head to the policeman, 'then the man must have known her. She was wearing a raincoat, so this chain, if there was one, must have been hidden from sight unless they were standing close together. And he must have had a torch. How else would he have seen it?'

'We had thought of that. But it could have been something in his possession, not hers.' Crombie prowled the summer house for a moment, leaves crunching beneath his feet, then said, 'All her regular boyfriends had alibis, but there's one young fellow who's out of town at the moment. We still need to have a word with him. Yes, Mrs Roberts?' he added as Karen suddenly sat upright. 'You've remembered something else?'

'If there was a chain round her neck when I found her, but none when Leigh got to her five or ten minutes later, then whoever killed her must still have been there, hidden in the bushes.' She felt the trembling start up again. 'I must have surprised him, and when I ran for help he took the chain because it incriminated him. He was there all the time!'

'Stop it, Karen! Put it out of your mind.' Leigh pulled her close again and said to Crombie, his voice hard and cold, 'Don't you think you've upset her enough for one day?'

'I'm afraid, sir, that it's part of my job to find out all I can. If the man was there, Mrs Roberts, you came to no harm and that is what you have to remember. And now, I think I've taken up enough of your time.'

Leigh kept his arm about Karen all the way back to the house, and she was glad of his support. Joyce came out of the house as the three of them walked across the lawn, then hurried down the steps to meet them.

'Karen? Are you all right?'

'I'm fine,' she assured her aunt as Crombie went crunching off across the gravel to disappear into the bushes, taking the path that led to Leigh's house.

'Just as well I went to look for her, Joyce,' Leigh said grimly. 'He was badgering her, asking more questions.'

'No, he wasn't. We were just talking about the garden and

the summer house when I suddenly remembered something.'

'Remembered what?'

'Never mind, Joyce,' Leigh said. 'It wasn't important, and right now Karen needs a drink and a change of subject.'

They squabbled mildly over the choice of drink, and Karen won.

'This is lovely,' she said approvingly after her first sip of sherry.

'I still think that a brandy would have been better for you, in your state.'

'I'm not in a state; I'm absolutely fine. I think I must be getting tough, learning to roll with the punches.' She was sitting on the sofa with Joyce and he stood before the fireplace; now she smiled up at him. 'Brandy's for after dinner, not before lunch.'

'My papa always had a glass of brandy and a cigar after dinner,' Joyce recalled fondly. 'In his study, every night, and nobody was allowed to disturb him. My mamma used to say that she would be afraid to try, even if the house went on fire.' She finished her own sherry and got up. 'I'd better go and see if Anna needs any help.'

'Leigh,' Karen began tentatively when they were alone, 'about this idea of Grant's . . .'

'Don't tell me that he's been trying to get you on his side! He has, hasn't he?' Leigh accused her as heat came to Karen's face. 'Of all the nerve!'

'It has nothing to do with nerve. I'm the managing director and it's only right that I become involved in any new plans. That's what I want, remember?'

'Of course I remember; I'm the one who's been trying to help you to learn about the business. But with all due respect, my love, you need to walk before you can run where Fletcher and Company's concerned. And Roberts knows that. He also knows that the final decision will come from the board. He had no right to go whining to you.'

'He didn't whine,' Karen said sharply. 'I was interested in what he had to say at the last meeting and I asked him to explain it further.' She led the way into the living room, eager to keep her face averted in case his shrewd dark-blue eyes read her own, and spotted the lie. 'And I think that it sounds worthwhile,' she finished defiantly.

'It's romantic and impractical.'

'But—'

'Karen . . .' She had seated herself on one of the two sofas flanking the fire; now he sat beside her and took her hands in his. 'Right now, we have a healthy order book, which is wonderful given the current economic climate. The textile market is not having a good time right now, so we must make sure that we're keeping our customers happy. That has to be our main objective.'

'But surely a new cloth could help us to keep going.'

'But in order to test it we have to take machines off work already being done for regular clients and use them for an experiment that might turn out to be a total failure.'

'Grant said that he could manage with just one machine.'

'And I don't think we can spare even one. Not right now. Next year, perhaps, but not now.'

She opened her mouth to argue, and then closed it again. He was adamant, and she had tried her best.

'The thing is, darling, you're still too new to this game to make major decisions.' Then, with a heart-warming grin: 'But if you're willing to put yourself in my hands, I'll turn you into an expert businesswoman in no time. In fact' – he drew her towards him – 'why don't you put yourself in my arms and I'll do my best to make you a happy businesswoman as well?'

She relaxed against him, returning his kisses, letting go of all responsibility. At least she would be able to tell Grant truthfully that she had tried.

'Marry me, Karen,' he said when they finally drew apart. 'I mean it. You need someone by your side at a time like this.'

'You're already by my side and so are Joyce and Anna and . . .'

He kissed the end of her nose. 'I mean someone of your

own, to look after you. Let's get married as soon as we can. Sooner, if possible.'

'I'm still married, remember?'

'Then get a divorce. What's stopping you?' He kissed her nose again. 'Just say yes and we'll keep it a secret until we can tell the world.'

Karen was tempted to give in. As Charlie had pointed out, Leigh was a very important part of her life. She didn't know what she would have done without him over the months since her father's death and the breakdown of her marriage; but at the same time she knew that she needed to straighten her life out before linking it with someone else's.

'Let me get through the divorce first, Leigh.'

'But, sweetheart . . .' he began; then: 'If that's what you want.'

'It is,' she said, as Joyce came in to tell them that lunch was ready.

Throughout the meal Joyce dominated the talk with an interminable discussion on the dead maid's background. She was convinced that Helen had had a private life that, by her account of it, matched that of any glamorous film star.

Leigh and Karen suffered the avalanche of words in silence, occasionally sharing a resigned glance across the table, and it fell to Anna to say sharply, 'She was just an ordinary lass, Miss Joyce, with an ordinary life, and nobody had any right to take it from her. So maybe it's time to stopping picking over what happened and why it happened, and let her rest in peace.'

'I sometimes feel that Anna's getting a little too familiar,' Joyce said when the housekeeper had left the room. Since Leigh was there, Anna had insisted on laying the dining-room table. Normally the three women ate together in the kitchen, but today the housekeeper was in the mood to be formal.

'She's family, Joyce,' Karen pointed out.

'No, she's not; she's the paid housekeeper,' her aunt snapped back at her, 'and it's time she realised that. Dan was far too lenient with her, and you're just the same.'

'Have you and Anna had a row?' Karen asked, surprised by the outburst. Her aunt drew herself up haughtily.

'Why would I quarrel with the hired help? I'm just telling you that she needs to be spoken to. Creeping around, snooping into things that don't concern her . . .'

'Are you saying that Anna has been looking through your private possessions, or mine?'

Joyce opened her mouth as though to launch into another tirade; then, as Leigh gave a polite little cough, as though reminding her of his presence as a guest, she subsided and said sulkily, 'I'm just saying that she's too familiar. Who knows what she does when we're both out and she's alone in the house?'

'I'm quite sure that Anna is as likely to pry into our possessions as we are to pry into hers, Joyce. She's always spoken her mind and, to be honest, I'd as soon we did as she suggested. Talking about what happened just brings it all back to me.' Karen shivered, remembering the dark path and the wind-lashed, rain-soaked trees whispering secrets all around her.

'Oh, darling!' Joyce reached across the table and took both Karen's hands in hers. 'How thoughtless of me. Nor another word, I promise!'

Twelve

K aren phoned Grant's office as soon as Leigh had gone: 'I need to speak to you.'

'I'll be here all afternoon, if you want to . . .'

'Could we meet in the coffee shop? In an hour?'

'If you prefer that.'

It was market day and the popular coffee shop was crowded, but Grant had arrived first and managed to claim a table by the window. He got to his feet when she came in, signalling to the waitress. Then, as soon as the woman had taken the order and left: 'Have you talked to Leigh about the cloth?'

Karen bit her lip. 'I tried, but he still doesn't like the idea. He says that the order book's busy and we have to honour promises made to loyal clients. And I can see the sense of that.'

His smile vanished and his face darkened. 'But this new idea can't wait for ever; surely you told him that?'

'I tried, but . . .'

'You're the main shareholder, for pity's sake, the executive director. You can overrule him – any of us – if you really want to. I thought you were keen to become more involved in what happened to the company?'

'I am, but—'

'And when your first real chance to make a difference comes along, what happens? You blow it.'

'Look,' Karen began, then stopped as the waitress said timidly, 'Er . . . two coffees?'

Grant scowled at her, and when their order was on the table he pulled a note from his pocket and thrust it at her.

'I'll just get your—'

103

'I don't want any change,' he snapped, and the woman scuttled off. Watching, Karen saw her murmur to another waitress, who turned to glance over at their table.

'Great, now it'll be all over town that we're still fighting.'

'You're not really interested in the business, are you?'

'I am! But I'm in a vulnerable position – you must see that.'

'Did you tell Bailie that I had your backing?'

'I said that I thought the project sounded worthwhile.'

'Worthwhile? That's big of you. So you're really on his side.'

Karen picked up her coffee cup, then put it down again when she realised that her hand was shaking. 'I'm not on anyone's side.'

'You didn't tell Bailie that you wanted me to try out the cloth.'

'No, and I'm not telling you that you can't do it. I'm not taking sides. You'll have to wait a little longer, Grant. Give me until the next board meeting; that's just two weeks away.'

He opened his mouth to argue, then hesitated, and shrugged. 'It doesn't look as though I have much choice, does it?'

'I'm sorry.' She almost reached out to touch his hand, but stopped herself when she saw that it was clenched so tightly on the table that the knuckles were as white as the snowy cloth. 'I'll speak up for you then, I promise. Your coffee's getting cold.'

'I'm not really interested in the coffee. As a matter of fact I'm pretty busy this afternoon, so if you don't mind . . .'

'Wait,' Karen said as he began to push his chair back. 'There's something else. You must have known about the offer for the company.'

'Yes, of course; we all did. But that's history now.'

'Not to me. I've just found out about it.'

'Yes, Edith told me you'd got the whole story out of her this morning.'

'Did she? There are no secrets between the two of you, are there?'

He raised an eyebrow. 'We're good friends, and colleagues. I respect her. And I believe that she also told you that the board turned the offer down while you were in hospital.'

'Yes, but the thing is: why would I want to sell?'

'Why not? You had no interest in the business – never have had.'

'Things have changed now.'

'I've still to see proof of that,' Grant said stiffly. He started to get up again and then stopped as she put a hand on his arm.

'The thing is . . . could my original decision to sell be enough to make someone want to prevent it?'

'Are you seriously suggesting that someone tried to kill you just to stop you letting Fletcher's go?'

'Not necessarily to kill me. Perhaps whoever it was only hoped to persuade me to change my mind. And when I refused . . .'

'Isn't that a bit melodramatic? Which of us do you suspect? Me? Edith? Forbes, maybe. Not Leigh, that's for sure. Not now that the two of you are getting back together again,' he mocked, and she felt herself go red.

'Grant, be serious!'

'If I was serious I would probably have to accept that I'm the major suspect.'

'Don't be ridiculous!'

His eyes were cold again. 'What's ridiculous about it? I'm the wicked husband, the one you want rid of so that you and Leigh can get on with your lives.'

'But—'

'If I was you, Karen, I would be very careful. If you insist on going around talking about this fantastic theory of yours to all and sundry, you might end up mentioning it to the wrong person. Then you could be in danger. Though I very much doubt that there's a word of truth in it. Now, I really do have to go.'

'Grant, sit down and listen to me . . .'

'I'm busy. But there's just one more thing. Do me a favour, will you? Do us all a favour.' He scowled down on her. 'Grow up!'

As he walked out, several pairs of eyes followed him and then, bright with greedy interest, swivelled back to stare at Karen.

With Helen's murder only two weeks in the past, the firm's annual dance was an ordeal for Karen. She and Joyce arrived in Leigh's car to find Forbes and Charlie already there, with Edith. Belinda arrived soon after, gorgeous in a tight-fitting black dress that offset her fair beauty. Seeing Leigh and Karen sitting together, she made at once for the empty chair on Leigh's other side.

'Isn't Grant with you?' Edith wanted to know.

'He's fussing round the car; he'll be here in a minute. Oh, I love this music. Let's dance, Leigh.'

'I was just about to ask Karen,' he began.

'I'd rather wait for a while,' Karen said swiftly, and Leigh was immediately claimed and whisked on to the dance floor, making an apologetic face at Karen over his partner's head.

'She makes it rather obvious, doesn't she?' Charlie asked, grinning. 'Did you catch that scowl she gave you, Karen?'

'That's the way Belinda always looks at me.'

'What's her problem?' Charlie began, and then subsided, nudging Karen as Grant arrived at the table.

It was the first time he and Karen had met since their public row in the coffee shop a few days earlier. He greeted her with a cool nod, and asked Edith to dance.

'I tell you, there's something going on between those two,' Charlie murmured as they moved away.

'According to Grant, they're friends and colleagues and he admires her.'

'Oh, isn't that sweet? Bless them!'

'You're wicked, Charlie Leslie.'

'I tell her that all the time,' Forbes agreed, 'but she never listens.'

His wife grinned at him. 'That's the kind of girl I am. Dance with me, my love.'

He hesitated, glancing at Karen, who pushed her chair

back. 'Go ahead. I have to get the mingling bit over and done with.'

She made a point of touring the crowded hall and talking to everyone, as Dan had always done. Some of the men asked her to dance, and she moved about the floor without hearing the music, concentrating on keeping a smile on her face and a light note in her voice. Then she returned to the table, from where first Forbes and then Leigh led her on to the dance floor.

Finally Grant had no option but to offer her his hand. Once, they had danced well together, but now they moved into the rhythm stiffly, each anxious to keep space between them.

'Look,' he said at last, above her head, 'I'm sorry I lost my temper with you when we met for coffee.'

'That's all right. We were both at fault.'

She heard him catch his breath as though about to say something else; but whatever it was, he decided against it. It was weird, Karen thought as they circled the floor in silence, to think that once upon a time all they had ever wanted was to be in each other's arms, be it on the dance floor or in bed. And now they were strangers. The thought made her lose track of the music, and she stumbled, feeling his arms tighten as she fell against him.

'Sorry.' She drew back hurriedly. 'Clumsy of me.'

'You're tired. Perhaps you should think of going home. You've done your bit and the evening's halfway through now.'

'I think I will.' She was definitely beginning to wilt and the dull headache that had been her constant companion in the first weeks after the attack was lurking in the background.

Grant began to steer her back to their table. 'I'll drive you back.'

'Leigh's already offered,' Karen said, and then, as they reached the others, 'I think I should leave before I cast a gloom over the proceedings. Would you mind, Leigh?'

He was already on his feet, reaching out to encircle her with his arm, drawing her away from Grant's side. 'Of course not. You look exhausted.'

'Yes, you do, darling,' Joyce fretted, 'and I promised Anna that I'd chase you off home as soon as you began to look tired.'

Belinda glared. 'Can't Forbes drive you home, Karen? Or what about a cab?'

'I'm taking her home and handing her over to Anna personally,' Leigh told her firmly.

'But I thought we were going to have the next dance.'

'The night is young yet. I'll be back before you know it.'

'You'd better be.' She reached out and touched his wrist with a brief, possessive gesture. Tired though she was, Karen winced inwardly as she saw it, and then she told herself that she was being ridiculously jealous.

'You should have stayed with Belinda,' she protested as Leigh guided her out into the blessedly cool, quiet, smoke-free night.

'Why, when I'd rather be with you?' he said, and the jealousy began to fade.

'If looks could have killed back there, I'd be dead.' The very word brought back memories she was trying to blank out, and she shivered. Leigh put an arm about her.

'Don't let her bother you; I certainly don't.'

'I think she's in love with you.'

He laughed, opening the car's passenger door for her. 'My darling, Belinda doesn't love anyone but herself.'

'You're very hard on her.'

'No, I'm being honest. Haven't you noticed that she has no time for women at all?'

'She certainly has no time for me, but that's because I took Grant away from the family circle.'

He closed the passenger door, and then said, when he had come round the car and was settling into the driving seat, 'And now she's looking daggers at Edith, because she and Grant seem to be getting quite close.' She was aware of him giving a sidelong glance in the darkness. 'You don't mind me saying that, do you?'

'Why should I?'

'I know that Edith's quite a bit older than he is,' Leigh said as he eased the car through the car park, 'but she's a very attractive woman.'

'We were talking about Belinda, and your neglect of her,' Karen reminded him, and he chuckled.

'Belinda is spoiled. She wants to be the centre of every man's attention, even her own brother's.'

'I noticed that when Grant and I were married. And now,' Karen said bleakly, 'she sees me as a threat where you're concerned.'

He laughed softly in the darkness. 'My darling Karen, Belinda isn't even in the running where I'm concerned.'

'But she's on the list of people with good reason to bear a grudge against me.'

'What are you talking about?'

'Oh, just that I've been collecting some very interesting stories lately.' Without meaning to, Karen began to tell him about Charlie's teenage resentment and Edith's love for her father having to be held in check because he hadn't wanted anyone else to come between him and his precious daughter.

'I suspected about Dan and Edith a long time ago, of course, though she and I have never mentioned it. But I would say that she's too strong a person to bear a grudge. And the same goes for Charlie.'

'Then there's Joyce, being dragged back home and having to give up her acting career to look after me . . .'

'Joyce loves you. We all do.' Briefly, he took his hand off the wheel to squeeze her fingers. 'Especially me. You can't possibly have me on that silly list of yours.'

'I broke off our engagement to marry Grant, remember?'

'But that's over, isn't it? I may have lost you temporarily, Karen, but now I have everything I want. Believe me, I'm too happy to bear any grudges.' He switched on the car radio; a woman with a smoky voice was singing a dreamy love song. 'If you ask me, your imagination's going haywire because you're overtired. By the way, I've called a special board meeting for the day after tomorrow. Could you be there, please?'

'What's it about? Is something wrong?'

'All in good time, and don't worry; it's just a small thing and we can sort it out in one meeting. Now, go to sleep, princess, and I'll waken you with a kiss when we reach your palace.'

Karen closed her eyes and leaned her head against the back of her seat. She was almost asleep when the car lurched crazily, throwing her violently against the door. She cried out and heard Leigh cursing as he struggled with the wheel; then the seat belt tightened, holding her as the car slewed round with a frightening scream of rubber on tarmac. The jolting, bucking sensations seemed to last for ever, but finally the car came to a standstill, tipped slightly to one side.

'Karen? Oh God, Karen . . . ?'

'I'm . . . I'm all right. What happened?' Somewhere in the darkness she heard Leigh struggling with his seat belt.

'I don't know. We've come off the road. Look, you stay still and I'll get out then free you.'

He managed to force his door open and disappeared into the darkness. She heard him crashing about, and then cursing.

'Leigh?'

'It's all right; we're in a ditch and I got soaked. Won't be a minute. Just wait there until I get to you.'

But Karen, with visions of the petrol tank leaking, possibly bursting into flames and turning the car into a fire-bomb, was already fumbling with her own seat belt. It came free surprisingly easily, and when she threw herself against the door it opened. She almost fell out, felt the shock of icy water as one foot plunged into it, and then managed to struggle to the roadside.

'Karen!' Leigh had come round the back of the car; now she heard him scramble after her.

'It's all right, I'm not hurt. There's someone coming,' she said joyfully as lights scythed the darkness, swung over the sky, then became two glowing eyes as a car turned the corner and headed towards them. Stepping into the road she snatched her gauzy scarf off and waved it.

'For God's sake, d'you want them to run you down?' Leigh caught her arm and pulled her back.

'I don't mind, as long as they see us. And they do!' she said thankfully as the oncoming car began to slow. Turning, seeing Leigh's car at a crazy angle in the ditch, she began to realise just how fortunate they had been. 'If you hadn't managed to stop in time,' she said shakily, 'if this had happened just round the next corner, we could have gone down the embankment and into the river . . .'

He put his arms around her, turning her away from the sight. 'But we didn't,' he said into her hair as the other car stopped and the driver and passenger began to scramble out. 'We're all right; we're safe. You're safe, and that's all that matters . . .'

Thirteen

'Now what?' Anna asked when she saw the two of them on the doorstep, wet and dishevelled, and with Karen wrapped in Leigh's coat. 'Was that a dance or a bunfight you went to?'

At least, Karen thought gratefully as Leigh helped her into the hall, Joyce was still at the dance, and not at home to fuss and fret over them.

'There's been an accident, Anna,' he was explaining tersely. 'The wheel came off my car and we were tipped into a ditch; but we're both all right, though Karen's a bit shaken. I think she should get to bed. And best to say nothing when Joyce comes home – leave it to the morning. I'm going back to the dance. I said I would, and I'm perfectly all right,' he added as Karen began to protest. 'I'll have to phone for a taxi, though. I'll tell them that I got a burst tyre.'

One of Anna's great virtues was the ability to act rather than speak when the occasion demanded. 'I'll run a hot bath,' she said now, 'and switch your electric blanket on.'

As she bustled off, Leigh went to the phone, dialled, and spoke briefly before hanging up. 'A car will be here in a few minutes.'

'Leigh . . .'

'Sshhh.' He drew Karen to him and dropped a kiss on her forehead. 'I'll come over in the morning. We can talk about it then. In the meantime, just you make sure that you have a good night's sleep.'

She nodded, and for several minutes they stood together, in each other's arms, without speaking. Then the sound of a horn outside heralded the taxi's arrival just as Anna arrived to announce that the bath was ready.

'I've put some lavender in it. Have a good soak while I get some soup heated up.'

'I don't want—'

'Yes, you do.' Anna shooed Karen towards the bathroom.

The soup was delicious, and so was the huge mug of hot chocolate to follow. Anna insisted on giving Karen two aspirin before she got into bed.

'There's nothing wrong with me!'

'From where I'm standing, young lady, there's something very wrong. I know that I said you were accident-prone, but this is going too far. What next, I wonder.'

'So do I.' Karen had intended to accompany the words with a wry smile, but to her horror and astonishment her face seemed to go out of control, and before she knew it she was sobbing uncontrollably on the housekeeper's sturdy shoulder.

'There, there now,' Anna repeated over and over again, easing them both on to the bed, where she rocked Karen as though she was a baby. 'Just you cry it all out, my lovely. It'll make you feel better.'

When the tears had eased to a series of hiccups, she mopped her employer's hot wet face then said, 'Best get into bed before Miss Joyce comes home. I'll tell her that you're sleeping like a lamb and not to be disturbed.'

Karen, exhausted and limp, climbed into bed and, as Anna tucked her in, she was reminded strongly of her childhood, when the housekeeper had represented safety and warmth and cosy routine.

'Oh Anna!' she burst out impulsively. 'It's so different now . . . it's all so wrong!'

'Don't you fret yourself, my pet. Everything will be all right, you'll see.'

'Will it? Will anything ever be right again? I can't stand it much longer – I can't!'

The housekeeper stood up, her face grim. 'I know, my lamb; you've had a right nasty time of it and now it has to stop.

Loyalty can only go so far and mebbe now the time's come for things to be said.'

'That's the trouble: I don't think I've been loyal to anyone. And what things have to be said?' Karen was confused.

'Not you, pet; you've been loyal enough. It's others that need to get themselves sorted out. Things have gone far enough and there needs to be an end to it. Now you dry your eyes and go to sleep. I'll leave the little lamp on.' She crossed to the French windows, drew the curtains aside, and tested the lock. 'They're well locked, so you've no need to fret about that. I'll look in from time to time in case you need me.'

Then she left, closing the door noiselessly behind her and Karen, drained of tears and energy, fell asleep almost at once.

'This is getting to be a habit,' Karen said as she limped into the kitchen at noon the next day to find Leigh, Grant and Edith with Joyce.

'It's you.' Anna, with help from Edith, was setting out plates of sandwiches and pouring tea and coffee. 'You never used to be so accident-prone. And your friends all care about you.'

Leigh, who, like Karen, was moving stiffly, came to take her hands in his.

'How are you?'

'I feel as though I've been through a mincing machine, but there's nothing that a bit of exercise won't cure.'

'I still think you should have let me send for the doctor,' Joyce worried. 'You might have internal injuries . . .'

'I haven't, so stop trying to frighten me.' Karen looked at the dark bruise on Leigh's cheekbone. 'You came off worse than I did.'

'I banged my face on the door frame when the car spun round. Did you sleep well?'

'Surprisingly well.' She freed her hands. 'What about the car?'

'One of the wheels had come off.'

'How the hell did that happen?' Grant wanted to know.

'Your guess is as good as mine.'

'And my guess is that it wasn't an accident.'

'For pity's sake, Karen,' Grant said wearily, 'you're not going to start that nonsense again!'

'As Anna said, I never used to be so accident-prone. Someone has to be behind all these things that are happening to me.'

'But who would want to hurt you?' Edith wanted to know. 'And why?'

'That's what I want to know.' A car drew up outside, and Karen glanced out of the window. 'There's going to one more for lunch, Anna. I phoned Inspector Crombie when I got up.'

'Don't bother telling anyone, will you?' Anna grumbled as she went to open the front door.

'Karen, you've had a rough time of it lately, but that could happen to anyone.' Edith's voice was calm and reasonable. 'Don't start reading something sinister into a series of isolated incidents.'

'Isolated?' Karen heard her own voice begin to rise. 'An intruder at the cottage, then again in my bedroom; poor Helen strangled and then Leigh's car going off the road last night. If you ask me . . .' She stopped short as Sam Crombie walked into the room.

'Please go on, Mrs Roberts,' the policeman invited.

'I was just saying that last night's car accident might not have been an accident.'

'It's like a television play, isn't it?' Grant said. 'All the suspects gathered together, and you've been invited as well, Inspector. The audience has gathered, and all we need now is the name of the murderer.'

Edith put a restraining hand on his arm, while Leigh snapped, 'That's enough, Grant.' Then, turning to Crombie: 'I'm glad to see you, Inspector, because I think Karen might well be right. I haven't had the report from the garage yet, but I suspect that my car was tampered with last night.'

Joyce whimpered and sagged back in her chair while relief swept through Karen.

'You believe me? You know that someone's trying to kill me?'

'Perhaps' – Leigh put his arm about her so that they faced the others together – 'someone tried to kill me. Or both of us.'

'We won't know for sure until the car's been checked, but if Mr Bailie's right . . . why would someone want to harm you, Mrs Roberts?' Crombie asked an hour later. The others had gone, and they were alone in the living room.

'That's the problem: I don't know. Until a few weeks ago I would have said that there wasn't a cloud on my horizon, but now everything's different.'

'Let's concentrate on last night. How did you get to the dance, and who was in your party there?'

'Leigh Bailie took my aunt and me there. We sat at a table with Forbes Leslie, the company's sales manager, and his wife, Grant and Belinda, and Edith Carpenter.'

'Who was there when you arrived?'

She frowned, trying to remember. It seemed like years ago instead of just last night. 'The Leslies and Edith Carpenter. Belinda Solomon arrived soon after, then Grant.

'Were you all together throughout the evening?'

'No, not at all. We're all expected to mingle at these staff occasions, and that's what we did.'

'So anyone at that dance could have gone into the car park in the dark, and tampered with Mr Bailie's car.'

'I suppose so, but so could anyone from outside. The whole town knew that the firm's annual dance was being held there that night.'

'Had it been arranged in advance that Mr Bailie would drive you home afterwards?'

'Because of this' – she put a hand up to the scar on her forehead – 'they all knew that I would probably leave early. Leigh had already offered to take me home when I was ready. Then Grant offered, because I looked tired. If I had agreed to that I wouldn't even have been in Leigh's car.'

'So if it was tampered with, whoever did it was thinking of Mr Bailie.'

'Are you suggesting that Grant might have done it, expecting to drive me home himself?'

'I'm not accusing anyone,' Crombie said swiftly.

'I can't believe that of Grant, or any of them. If I have an enemy, it has to be the man who attacked me at the cottage!'

'Mrs Roberts, why would a complete stranger take the trouble to follow up an assault?'

'He might, if he thought that I could identify him, or knew something he didn't want me to remember. That's what I've been trying to tell the others, but they wouldn't believe me. Do you?'

'I have no reason to disbelieve you, Mrs Roberts. By the way, we've interviewed your maid's current boyfriend. He was supposed to meet her that night, and he confirmed that she often cut through the shrubbery and then down Mr Bailie's driveway to meet him further along the road; but as it turns out, he wasn't at the meeting place that night. He had gone out on his motorbike with friends that day and met with an slight accident, so he was in a hospital casualty department fifty miles away when she met up with her killer.' He got to his feet. 'I'll keep in touch; thank you for the lunch. And don't worry,' he added kindly: 'we'll get to the bottom of this business. I promise you that.'

But soon enough, Karen wondered when she was alone, to save her life?

Leigh phoned that evening, his voice sombre. 'Karen, the garage mechanic reckons that someone loosened that wheel deliberately.' The final word fell into her ear like a stone and she shivered, though the hall was warm enough.

'Have you told . . . ?'

'Crombie? He came to the garage with me. Are you all right?' he asked, concern thawing his voice. 'Do you want me to come over?'

'No, I'm fine, and I want an early night anyway.'

'If you're certain . . .'

'I am. And Leigh, don't say anything to Joyce about this. She'll only worry.'

'She's not the only one, but I know what you mean. No sense in frightening her, and now that Crombie knows about the wheel he'll keep an eye out for the two of us.' Then, becoming businesslike: 'You haven't forgotten tomorrow's meeting, have you?'

'Couldn't you put it off for a few days?'

'No, it's important, and I need you to be there, Karen. I need your support. I'll collect you at—'

'No need; I'll drive myself.'

'If you're sure.'

'I am.'

'Very well. In the meantime, try to get a good night's sleep, darling,' he said, and hung up.

'Who was that?'

Startled, Karen whirled round, almost dropping the telephone. 'Oh, Joyce; you made me jump! It was only Leigh, reminding me about the special meeting he's called for tomorrow.'

'Are you sure you feel up to it?'

'I'll be all right,' Karen assured her aunt; then, as a faint throbbing began in the region of the scar she still bore on her forehead: 'But I think I'll have an early night, just to make sure. And could I have one of your sleeping pills, please?'

By the time Karen reached the office the others were waiting in the boardroom to start the meeting. The first thing she noticed when she went in was the way the air seemed to crackle as though charged with electricity. Grant's eyes were stormy, and he fidgeted incessantly with the file before him, while Edith gave Karen a quick, mechanical smile and then stared down at the polished table. Forbes looked uncomfortable and Leigh scarcely gave Karen time to take her place at the head of the table before opening the meeting.

He began by speaking of the heavy commitments facing the

118

firm, delivery dates to be met and problems incurred because one of the machines had had to be taken out of service.

'It required maintenance, or so we were led to believe. But only two days ago I discovered by pure chance that the machine's not faulty at all. In fact, it's working overtime on an unauthorised project – a project that we had all agreed to shelve for further discussion.' He paused, his eyes fixed on Grant, who stared back at him, eyebrows raised slightly. 'But it would seem that the board's decisions count for little as far as some of its members are concerned,' Leigh resumed, his voice hard. 'You might want to say a few words at this point, Grant, in your own defence.'

'I would just like to say—' Edith began, and then Grant broke in.

'Best to leave it to me, Edith.' Grant's tension had vanished, to be replaced by a slight smile. 'It's a fair cop, guv. You've got me bang to rights.'

'So you admit that you took the machine out of production to work on your pet project . . .'

'Of course. Why should I deny it? I gave Mike Ramsay permission to modify the machine and try out his new material, because as works manager I have a duty to do all that I can for Fletcher and Company.'

'As works manager you should have the integrity to go along with the board's decisions. You knew that we were prepared to consider this project in more detail at the next meeting!'

'And I also knew that, while Fletcher's seemed to be doing well enough as it is, you would never have the courage to try anything new. So we – I – decided that the best policy would be to give you a practical demonstration.'

'I think, Madam Chairwoman, that we should send for Ramsay and—'

'He acted on my instructions, Leigh, so don't think of crucifying him in order to appease your hurt pride.' Then, as Leigh's face whitened: 'Perhaps I'm not the only one who should remember that he's one of a group, not a tinpot dictator.'

'That's enough, Grant.' Forbes Leslie's normally placid voice carried a warning undertone and Grant gave him a long look, then shrugged and said, 'You're quite right. I apologise.'

'And you'll put the machine back into normal service?' Leigh insisted, and Grant gave another shrug.

'Certainly. It's served its purpose in any case. The first sample of cloth has been run and we already have a buyer who might be interested.'

'A buyer?' Forbes' voice cracked with astonishment.

'That's right, Forbes,' Edith said. 'I knew what Grant and Mike were doing and I told Teddington's about the new material. They're interested in seeing it.'

'You did all this behind our backs?' Forbes asked.

'I gave you the chance to co-operate but you weren't interested,' Grant told him.

'Grant's right, and I don't think it's fair to let him carry the blame for all of this.' Edith shot a faint smile across the table at Grant. 'I'm as guilty as he is.'

'I don't think it's a case of guilt,' Grant corrected her calmly. 'We did nothing wrong.'

'Nothing wrong?' Karen had never seen Leigh so angry. 'You've been plotting behind our backs!'

'I wanted to prove to you – all of you,' Grant said, his gaze taking in Karen as it swept around the table, '– that Ramsay has hit on a goldmine. There are samples in my office right now, if you care to see them.'

Leigh's fist crashed on the table and a notepad jumped. 'You had no right! You deserve to be thrown out of the firm for this!'

'If Grant goes, I go too,' Edith said quietly.

'Now hold on . . .' Forbes interrupted as Leigh's anger grew. 'Let's look at this rationally. The damage, if there was any damage, is done. Because one of the machines has been hijacked, we've fallen behind on an order, and you'll have to take the blame for that, Grant. It will be up to you to see that the order's completed on time and that we don't break faith with regular clients.'

'Of course. I'll work at the machines myself if necessary, day and night. Your order will go out on time – don't worry about that.'

'And it's up to you to convince us that this new idea is as good as you seem to think. If it isn't – well, as long as that order meets its deadline, there will be no harm done,' Forbes pointed out; and then, suddenly seeming to realise that he was laying down the law, he flushed, stammered, then turned hopefully to Karen. 'Do you agree, Madam . . . Kar— Mrs Roberts?'

Karen nodded. 'It sounds reasonable to me. Leigh?'

He glared at her, and then threw his pen down on the table. 'I suppose it's too late to do anything else. But if you ever go against the wishes of this board again, Roberts, I for one will be looking for your resignation.'

'Is that a threat?'

'For heaven's sake, you two, stop behaving like little boys squabbling over a toy!' Edith burst out. 'Karen – Madam Chairwoman – I propose that this meeting be closed so that we can all inspect the new material. Then we can discuss everything properly at next week's meeting.'

Weak with gratitude for Edith's intervention, Karen closed the meeting, walked quickly from the room before anyone could talk to her, and went straight out to her car.

Fourteen

She was huddled by the sitting-room fire an hour later, shivering despite the warmth of the flames, when Grant walked in.

'Go away,' she said flatly.

'I have to talk to you.'

'You should have talked to me earlier. You should have told me what you were up to.' Her hurt feelings spilled over. 'You said you were pleased about me wanting to become more involved in Fletcher's, then you went behind my back. You knew that I was trying to win Leigh round for you.'

'But you weren't getting very far, so I had to go ahead on my own.'

'Without telling me.'

'Would you have gone along with me if you'd known? You bet your sweet life you wouldn't,' Grant said. 'Besides, I didn't want to burden you with a guilty secret. I doubt if you would have been able to stop yourself from running to Leigh to tell him all about it.'

'So you confided in Edith instead.'

'Because she's an important part of the firm,' he said, and Karen felt a stab of jealous resentment against cool, dependable Edith. 'She understands about these things. She knows better than any of us how Dan would have reacted . . . she understood him.'

'Oh yes, she understood him very well, didn't she? She was very close to my father!' Her voice shook, and he gave her a long, level look.

'If you're about to start telling tales out of school, Karen,

122

don't bother. I know all about that. I've known since before we were married.'

'And you said nothing to me?'

'It was none of my business. Don't, for God's sake, take it out on Edith because she loved your father,' he said quietly. 'I thought you had more understanding, more compassion.' Then, when she refused to answer or to look at him: 'I needed a strong case to put in front of the board – Edith knew that. She was in a position to cover up for me, and to find a possible buyer. And it's worked.' He sat down in the chair opposite, leaning towards her, elbows on knees, his face lighting up. 'Forbes Leslie likes the new material, Karen. Even Leigh was impressed, though he tried hard to hide it. Why didn't you come along to my office with the others after the meeting?'

'I needed fresh air. My head . . .' It was a feeble excuse, and they both knew it.

'Was it because of the disagreement between Leigh and myself? You'll have to get used to that sort of thing; it's all part of the cut and thrust of business.'

'It looked like more than that to me.'

He shrugged. 'Bailie knows that the firm needs me as much as it needs him.'

'It needs you, it needs Leigh, it needs Edith and it needs Mike Ramsay. But it doesn't need me.' She got to her feet. 'I've tried to be more like my father, Grant – to become part of the firm. But it's no use. I just don't fit in. I don't know how to fit in. Perhaps that buyout offer we had was a good idea.'

'You'd sell out?' He was shocked, incredulous.

'Why not? I don't want to spend the rest of my life at board meetings, listening to you and Leigh turning the place into a bone of contention between you. It would be better to make a clean break.'

'No!'

'Oh don't worry,' she said tartly. 'You're a shareholder and an executive; you'd stay with it whoever took over. It wouldn't make much difference to anyone but me.'

'It would make a hell of a difference to a lot of people,

or are you too blinded by self-interest to see that?' He stood up. 'Business isn't about people, Karen; it's about profits. Have you never heard of asset-stripping? I suppose not.' He answered his own question scathingly as she opened her mouth to answer. 'You've never had to learn these things. You've always been protected from the nastier side of life.'

'Grant, I think you'd better go.'

'Not until I've had my say. You think that you can just walk away from your responsibilities and be happy ever after, but it doesn't work that way, sweetheart. Happiness only comes when you can cope with the downs of life as well as the ups; but whenever you meet a down, Karen, you run away from it, don't you? When marriage starts to seem too much like real life, walk away from it! When things get out too difficult, get rid of the factory and sell all the people in it down the river.'

'That is not true!'

'Oh yes it is. But you don't like hearing the truth, do you?' Grant pressed on mercilessly. 'You still think that everything will be perfect just around the corner. But it won't, Karen. It's time you learned to face up to life and cope with whatever it throws at you.'

'You have no right to speak to me like this!'

'That's not just a factory back there; that's people and years of hard work. Dan dedicated his life to developing it, and he did it for you, Karen. It fed you and clothed you and gave you a good life and a lot of standing in your home town. And now you're prepared to sell up as though it's a . . . a dress that you've grown tired of?'

'Don't moralise, Grant!' she snapped at him. 'And don't start that business about being a Fletcher; it didn't suit you the last time we had a row, did it? Then, I was a Roberts. All right, I'll be a Roberts. So what does the name Fletcher mean to me now?'

'You're the most twisted human being I have ever met!' His voice was thick with rage. He stormed across the room, his fingers digging into her shoulders as he spun her round to face him. 'I won't let you do this, Karen – I won't! I'll stop you if it's the—'

He stopped abruptly as the door opened.

'Mrs Roberts, can you spare a moment?' Sam Crombie enquired mildly. 'I don't want to interrupt . . .' he went on, as Grant released Karen. She turned to see the policeman standing on the threshold, with Joyce hovering behind him.

'Don't worry, Inspector; you weren't interrupting anything out of the ordinary,' Grant was saying behind her. 'Just a little marital discussion between my wife and myself. Joyce will tell you that that used to be a daily event in this house. Excuse me.'

Crombie stepped aside to let him pass, then closed the door gently on Joyce's worried face and came further into the room.

'Are you all right, Mrs Roberts?'

'Yes, of course. I'm sorry about . . .' She gestured helplessly towards the closed door.

He waved the apology aside. 'I called because . . . Mr Bailie told you about his car being tampered with?'

'Yes, but we've kept it from my aunt. I don't want her to worry.'

'What about your housekeeper?'

'Anna? She doesn't . . .' Karen began, and then paused, remembering Anna's words on the night of the accident: 'Mebbe now the time's come for things to be said.'

'Anna may know more than we think.'

He nodded. 'Sometimes outsiders who have been part of a family for years sees more than anyone else. And Miss Harper strikes me as a very shrewd lady. I think I'll have another word with her. Now, about the incident the other night. Can you think of any reason why anybody might want to harm Mr Bailie?'

'Why should anyone want to harm either of us?'

'My wife gets really annoyed with me sometimes,' Sam Crombie said unexpectedly. 'She says that I never listen to

125

her, and so I never know what's going on in my own family. True, of course. I think it's because I spend my working hours listening and even prying at times. Not something I enjoy, but it's part of the job. All of this is leading up to something. I must ask you, Mrs Roberts . . . about your relationship with your husband, and with Mr Bailie.'

Karen felt her face grow warm. 'It's really quite straightforward, Inspector. At one time I was engaged to Leigh Bailie. Then Grant came into the family business, and he and I . . .' It all seemed so long ago now. 'I broke off my engagement to Leigh and married Grant.'

'Was Mr Bailie resentful?'

'No, though he had every reason to be. When we became engaged he had bought the house next door so that I would still be near my father when we were married. We had set a date, when I met Grant. In his place, I would have been furious. But he and Grant liked each other, and Leigh was wonderful about it. He even spoke up for me when my father tried to get me to change my mind about Grant.'

'So your father didn't like the idea of you marrying Mr Roberts.'

'It was nothing to do with Grant; he was annoyed with the way I had treated Leigh. He felt that a promise made should be a promise kept. He only came round to the idea when he realised that Leigh didn't bear any grudges.'

'And now, as I understand it, things have come full circle and you and Mr Bailie will probably marry when your divorce comes through.'

'Everyone seems to think so, but we haven't committed ourselves to anything. It's too early to make plans.'

'How does Mr Roberts feel about that possibility?'

'It would be better to ask him, but I don't think he cares what I do. Our marriage was a mistake and we're both looking forward to gaining our freedom.'

'So that . . . disagreement . . . you were having when I came in didn't concern Mr Bailie?'

'What made you think it did?'

126

'Your husband was telling you that he would not let you do something,' he reminded her.

'And you thought we were arguing over Leigh? Good heavens, no! It was a disagreement over the family business,' she said, then, hurriedly, 'And Grant's bark has always been a lot worse than his bite. He didn't mean what he was saying.'

'So you wouldn't consider him capable of harming you or Mr Bailie.'

'Absolutely not!'

'Mmmm.' Crombie got up. 'I'll have a word with Miss Harper before I go. You know where to find me if you need me at any time.'

Karen accompanied him into the hall. As he disappeared into the kitchen the telephone began to shrill. She hesitated, reached out a hand to lift the receiver and then let it fall back to her side as Joyce hurried into the hall.

'If that's for me I'm not in, whoever it is.'

Her aunt darted a puzzled look at her as she spoke into the receiver. 'Hello? Oh, Leigh . . . well, she is . . .' she said indecisively; then under Karen's furious gaze she hurried on, 'but she's having a rest and I don't want to disturb her.'

Karen turned away and wandered into the living room. Joyce joined her a few minutes later, biting her lip.

'Darling, what is it? Leigh said there was a row at the meeting, and when the inspector arrived I was never so glad to see anyone in my life. Do you know that you and Grant were shouting? I really thought he was going to . . .' She stopped, horrified, then finished lamely, '. . . going to cause a terrible scene.'

'It's just office business, Joyce.'

'But why didn't you want to talk to Leigh?'

'I'm tired, that's all. I couldn't face another post-mortem. I think I'll lie down for a while.'

'I'll get Anna to make some tea.' Joyce was a great believer in the soothing powers of tea. She insisted on seeing Karen settled in her room and showered her with offers ranging from smelling salts to a new book, which she was reading herself. 'I don't mind letting you have it before I've finished; it might help to take your mind off things.'

'Joyce, it would take more than a good book to take my mind off things,' Karen said wearily.

Anna brought the tray into the bedroom, dumping it down on the bedside table with a clatter. 'If your father had been alive to hear that shouting match between you and Mr Roberts, he would have taken you across his knee and spanked some sense into you! I've never heard such goings-on.'

'Anna . . .'

'I've been here long enough to be able to speak my mind,' the older woman said huffily. 'The two of you were yelling at each other as though you had no sense at all – you're grown-up married people, for goodness' sake!'

'And soon we'll be divorced people – and now you know why!'

'I know that it's time you both got a grip of yourselves. Even divorce is no reason for shouting like that. You had love for each other once – and don't deny it, for it was there for all the world to see – so surely you can at least have a little respect for each other and not let yourselves down in front of that policeman.'

'You're right,' Karen admitted meekly. 'You're always right. Now why don't you go and give Grant a good talking-to as well?'

'Don't worry, I intend to.' Anna plumped up the pillows. 'That policeman's put me in a right bad mood, coming to the kitchen to ask me more questions.'

'He's not still here, is he?'

'He is not. I soon sent him off with a flea in his ear. He seemed to think I was hiding something from him.'

'Are you?'

Anna glared. 'If I know something that he should know, I'll tell him. And stop trying to change the subject. You're going to have to clear up this business quarrel. It'll only fester if you don't.'

128

Karen finished her tea and put the cup down. 'Perhaps you're right.'

'I am. You've got enough on your mind without dragging in more trouble. Now, have a bit of a lie down and you'll feel better.'

Belinda's face hardened when she opened the door of the flat to see Karen standing on the step.

'Well?' she asked ungraciously.

'Is Grant in?'

'You've got a nerve, coming here!' the other girl hissed at her.

For a moment Karen recoiled, then rallied. 'I own this house,' she reminded her sister-in-law coldly, 'and at least I paid you the courtesy of walking round to the side door.'

'That's you all over, isn't it? Just because you've got money you think you can walk all over the rest of us. How could you even think of selling Fletcher's when you know what that firm means to Grant and Leigh!'

'It means something to me as well, Belinda; but that has nothing to do with you.' Karen held her anger down, but she was aware that her fists were clenching by her side.

Belinda's smooth, pale skin was blotchy with anger. 'You never think of anyone but yourself, do you?'

'I came to speak to Grant.'

'He's not in,' Belinda said, and slammed the door.

Karen jammed her fists in her pockets and continued on round the house to where the car was parked outside the kitchen door. She got in, started the engine and roared off down the driveway, desperate to get away from everything and everyone.

Fifteen

'What's wrong?' Karen asked when she went into the kitchen on Sunday morning to find Anna banging pots around while Joyce sat at the table, her mouth turned down at the corners.

'Why should you think that anything's wrong?' Anna wanted to know. 'Helen's been murdered and we have police all over the place, and I'm working my fingers to the bone. Is that not what most folk are putting up with?'

'I thought I heard . . .'

'Thought you heard what?' Anna snapped. What Karen had heard, as she came through the hall, was a quarrel between the two women in the kitchen, and quite a vicious quarrel at that; but looking at the housekeeper's expressionless face and hooded eyes, she knew that there was no point in prying.

'Nothing.'

'Then you heard right, for there was nothing to hear. What do you want for your breakfast?'

'You sit down and I'll make it.'

'I'd as soon do it myself than have to clear up after you. I can manage.'

'I don't want anything,' Joyce said, and Karen looked from one to the other, then ventured to ask, 'Have you two had a row?'

'Servants,' Anna said flatly, 'can't have rows. Servants just have to do as they're told.'

'Oh for goodness' sake! Aunt Joyce, go into the dining room and I'll bring your breakfast in,' Karen said, exasperated. When her aunt had gone, she fetched a bowl and started breaking eggs into it. 'Do you want to tell me what that was all about?'

'No.' Anna folded her lips together, and would say no more. Nor would Joyce, when Karen took a tray to her.

Defeated, she stopped trying to prise information out of them, opting instead to stay home and help Anna while Joyce, as was her habit, went to church. During the morning she found time to phone Leigh.

'Can you come over for lunch . . . please? Joyce and Anna are at each other's throats today and I could do with some moral support.'

'I'd be delighted. What's bothering them?'

'The same thing that's bothering the rest of us, I think,' Karen said. 'Things are beginning to get us down.'

'I'm glad you phoned,' Leigh said when he arrived. 'I've not had a chance to see you alone for the past couple of days.'

'I needed some space.'

'Joyce told me that you and Grant had a row.'

'More of a disagreement.'

'According to Joyce things were getting pretty stormy when she and Inspector Crombie walked in on the two of you.' He hesitated, then said, 'Karen, I don't think that this is a good time for you and Grant to get involved in public arguments, particularly in front of the police.'

'My private life has nothing to do with the police, or with Helen's murder.'

'I know that, but even so, I think we should all present as united a front as possible until they catch whoever killed your maid.'

'Does that mean that there will be no more rows between you and Grant for the time being?'

'That', Leigh said evenly, 'was strictly business. We have no quarrel outside the office. And talking of business, let's not. Come out for a drive after lunch.'

'I don't know, Leigh. I'm not very good company these days.'

'You'll enjoy this trip. And don't invite Joyce along,' he

added as they heard the front door open. 'This outing will be limited to you and me.'

'She wouldn't want to come anyway; she's going to visit that invalid friend of hers this afternoon.'

'Good,' Leigh murmured, his hand caressing the nape of her neck and his breath warm on her cheek. 'That means that I'll get you all to myself.'

Then Joyce came in, her face lighting up at the sight of him.

Although Joyce and Anna were noticeably cool towards each other, Leigh's presence made lunch bearable for Karen, and the prospect of an outing afterwards helped.

Once in the car, Leigh took charge. 'Don't ask me to drive you anywhere in particular because I know where we're going . . . and don't ask,' he instructed her. 'Just sit back and enjoy yourself.'

'We're not visiting someone, are we?' Karen said, dismayed, when he finally swung the car in through double white gates and drew up before a small, comfortable manor house.

'Nope.'

'Are you thinking of moving?' She eyed the house, searching for a 'For Sale' sign.

'Would you miss me if I did?'

'Of course I would. Joyce and I rely on having you next door.'

'Don't worry, you'll not get rid of me as easily as that,' he assured her as he got out of the car then walked round to open the passenger door. As she got out, three dogs, all poodles, came rushing round the side of the house, then stopped short as a woman's voice called their names.

'Good afternoon, Mr Bailie.' An elderly woman in jeans and a jersey had followed the poodles. 'I thought I heard your car on the drive. Hello there . . . Mrs Roberts, isn't it? This way.'

Leigh took Karen's hand as they followed the woman to a large shed at the back of the house.

'You lot can just stay out here,' the woman said, ushering

132

her visitors in then closing the door on the poodles. 'There they are,' she added, pointing at a large dog basket, then stood back as Leigh drew Karen towards it.

'What d'you think, darling?'

'They're adorable!' She dropped to her knees to admire the squirming mass of sleepy black puppies. 'Just like Monty when we first got him!'

'He came from here too. All pedigreed stock. I didn't mean to bring you here for another couple of weeks, but since you're in need of some cheering up . . . which one would you like?'

'You mean . . . ?' She looked up at him with sudden alarm. 'Leigh, it's too soon.'

'No, it's not,' he told her. 'Monty was a very important part of your life, and I can't bear to see how you miss him. Anyway, I want to do this for you. Go on, choose one.'

'How old are they?'

'Just over three weeks,' the woman said. 'None of them is spoken for yet because I would normally wait for a few more days before advertising them, but Mr Bailie was very persuasive and so you have first choice.'

'Here . . .' Leigh picked up one of the pups and put it into Karen's hands. The plump little body was warm and silky, and as the puppy looked up at her she felt her heart turn over. She could not resist these adorable babies.

By the time they got into the car twenty minutes later it had been arranged that Leigh would collect one of the pups in three weeks' time.

'You're looking better already,' he said approvingly as they drove homewards. 'I knew that having another dog would be good for you.' Then, with a change of tone: 'You don't think that Grant will mind, me buying a pup for you? I've just realised that Monty was his wedding gift to you.'

'I doubt if Grant will be bothered, and in any case, it's not his business.'

'But Monty was more than a pet, wasn't he? He was a part of your marriage, almost like a symbol. Now the marriage has gone and he's gone too, poor little chap. It's almost as though there's a link.'

The afternoon's happiness took on a faint chill. 'You're not suggesting that Grant deliberately poisoned Monty because our marriage went sour, are you?'

'Good God, of course I didn't mean it that way.' Leigh took one hand off the steering wheel to give her knee a reassuring pat. 'And you're right, he won't mind.'

'I'm not so sure about Joyce and Anna though. It took them ages to get used to Monty. And we were living on the upper floor then, so they weren't too badly affected. It'll be different now that we're all on the ground floor.'

'We can keep the little fellow over at my house until he's house-trained and fit to meet them.'

'Not at all. If I'm to have a new dog, then I want him to be with me from the beginning. In any case, it's my house.'

'My own sentiments exactly. You worry too much about other people, Karen.'

'If you ask me, I haven't given enough thought to others in the past.'

'Nonsense! You're loved by a lot of people.'

'More than I deserve. I'm going to change from now on,' she announced as the car turned into her driveway.

'Don't change too much, will you? I'm very fond of you, just the way you are.'

'Oh, there's lots of room for improvement. For a start, I'm going to make it up to you for all the harm I caused.'

'What harm could you possibly have done to me?' Leigh asked as he stopped the car.

'I broke off our engagement so that I could marry Grant.'

For a second his face was wiped of all expression, and then he said easily. 'Darling, learn to put the past behind you, the way I have.'

'You're so good to me, Leigh.'

He took her hand and kissed it. 'Being good to someone like you comes easily.'

'You were wonderful, interceding with my father the way

you did, and getting him to see my point of view. I wish I could tell him how sorry I am about causing him all that grief,' she said soberly.

'On the other hand, he was spared the grief of seeing the two of you split up. And he would be pleased about us, wouldn't he?'

'Yes, of course. Come in and have a cup of coffee. You can help me to break the puppy news to Anna, and to Joyce if she's back. I remember,' Karen went on as she opened the door and led the way into the house, 'the time Monty managed to find his way downstairs, a few days after we got him. He started swinging on the hall curtains, and by the time Anna found him he had managed to chew several little holes in the hem. She marched upstairs holding him out at arm's length, her face like—'

Looking back afterwards, she had no clear recollection of what happened next. One minute she was walking in through the door, intent on her story, and the next she was at the bottom of the wide, graceful staircase, kneeling beside the figure sprawled on the floor.

'Anna?' Then: 'Leigh . . . !'

She held one hand up to him, the fingers that had automatically brushed grey hair back from the housekeeper's hidden face streaked by bright streamers of blood.

Then, hearing a gasp from the upper floor, she looked up to see Belinda standing at the top of the stairs, clinging to the railings, her face as white as a sheet.

'I had just come in,' Belinda said several hours later, her voice shrill with tension. 'I heard Karen's voice calling, so I went to the top of the stairs and then I saw . . .' She put a hand to her mouth and Leigh, sitting on the arm of her chair, put an arm about her.

They had all – Karen and Joyce, Leigh and Grant – spent several hours in the small hospital waiting room, only to be told that it would be some time before the housekeeper recovered consciousness . . . if at all. Restless, not knowing what to do, they had gathered in the living room, to be joined by Belinda. Karen and Joyce had made sandwiches and coffee, but nobody had much of an appetite.

'If only I had been here.' Karen's voice broke on the last few words. 'If only we hadn't left her on her own.' When tears began to trickle down her face, Joyce took her hand and held it tightly.

'Oh darling, don't blame yourself. Even if the house had been filled with people, Anna could still have missed her footing and fallen down the stairs.'

'I still say that someone should be at the hospital in case . . . when Anna comes round.' Grant was pacing the floor. 'She might be disorientated; she needs to have a familiar face there.'

'The hospital people said that they would let us know if we were needed,' Joyce said, to Karen as much as to Grant. 'We can be there within fifteen minutes. Leigh, more coffee?'

'I can manage.'

'Let me; I need to have something to do.' Joyce gave Karen's hand a final pat then went to take Leigh's coffee cup. 'It's my fault,' she fretted as she poured coffee then began to spoon sugar into the cup. 'I was the last to leave the house. And I've been taking Anna for granted . . . that poor, poor woman! I should have realised that she was beginning to get a bit shaky . . .'

'Thank you, Joyce, I'm fine for sugar now.' Leigh stayed her hand as she dipped the spoon into the bowl for the fourth time.

'We just don't notice people growing old, do we?' she swept on, 'not when they're living under the same roof.'

'That's nonsense.' Grant's voice was brusque. 'Anna's as fit as a fiddle; she's probably no older than you are, Joyce.' Then, oblivious to the look Joyce gave him: 'She tripped on the stairs, that's all.'

'But how could that happen? The carpet's quite new, and Anna always wears sensible shoes. I can't see how she could have caught her heel on anything.'

'For goodness' sake, Karen, don't start going all neurotic again,' Belinda said waspishly. Then she stared as Leigh cut in: 'I'm not so sure that Karen's being neurotic.'

'You're surely not going to suggest that the woman was pushed, are you? Was she pushed, or did she jump?' Belinda declaimed melodramatically.

'That's not in very good taste,' Leigh told her sharply; and then, as Karen's teaspoon clattered noisily into her saucer: 'Are you all right, Karen? You look terribly pale.'

'I'm . . . yes.' Karen's mouth was so dry that her tongue seemed twice its usual size. 'It's just the thought of someone deliberately pushing Anna downstairs. Why would anyone want to hurt her?'

'My point exactly.'

'But a lot has been going on around here recently,' Leigh persisted. 'The cottage incident, the maid's murder – and nobody can claim that that was an accident – then the wheel came off my car, and now this.'

'And Monty was poisoned,' Karen put in.

'Oh yes, let's not forget the dog.' Like many pretty women, Belinda could look quite ugly when she scowled. 'Stop trying to make five by adding two and two together, Leigh. Anna either stumbled on the stairs or she took some sort of dizzy turn. It's as simple as that.'

'She's been working too hard lately, without anyone to help her since Helen's . . . since poor Helen was . . . oh, dear,' Joyce said miserably, 'it's all so terrible!'

'And trying to read something into a domestic accident doesn't help!'

'That's enough, Belinda,' Grant ordered.

'But she's insinuating that one of us deliberately hurt Anna. Are you saying that you think that I tried to hurt her, Karen? Or perhaps it was Leigh – oh no, you two can give each other alibis, can't you, since you spent the afternoon together.' Venom gave added sparkle to Belinda's green eyes. 'Perhaps it was Joyce or Grant . . .'

'I said, that's enough,' her brother cut in. He slammed his

coffee cup down so hard that it jangled in its saucer, and moved quickly across the large room to take his sister by the wrist, pulling her up from her chair.

'You're hurting!'

'And you're hurting the people who care about Anna,' he told her savagely. 'I think we should be going upstairs, don't you?'

'Wait a minute,' Leigh interrupted. 'I imagine that we're going to hear from Inspector Crombie soon, and he'll want know what we were all doing this afternoon when Anna fell. What are you going to tell them, Belinda?'

'Me?' As Grant released her, Belinda rubbed her wrist, disconcerted by the turn the conversation had taken. 'As it happens, I went across to your house. I thought that we might spend the afternoon together, but you weren't there. You had gone out with Karen.' Again her sullen gaze raked them both.

'How do you know I was with Karen?'

'You came into the house together, didn't you? Are you telling me that you met on the doorstep, or . . .' Her eyes narrowed. '. . . that one of you was already in the house?'

'We did spend the afternoon together, as it happens. I only wanted to point out that people sometimes misunderstand what they see, or hear,' Leigh told her smoothly. 'What did you do after calling at my house?'

'I went for a walk, and before you ask, I was on my own and I didn't see anyone I knew.'

'Grant?'

'I don't see that it's any of your business.'

Leigh shrugged. 'If you prefer to wait until the police question you, that's fine. It would certainly give you more time to think of what you're going to say,' he pointed out, and Grant flushed.

'I was in the office, clearing up some work. And like Belinda, I was alone. Nobody else saw me there.'

'And as you know, I was with Mrs Blair all afternoon,' Joyce said swiftly as Leigh turned to look at her. 'You all know that I usually pop over to keep her company on a Sunday afternoon.'

'Which means,' Belinda said triumphantly, 'that Anna was alone in the house. And she fell, by accident.'

'There's one thing we haven't considered yet.' Karen ignored the faint rustle that went around the room. 'What was Anna doing on the stairs in the first place? Was she on her way up when she fell, or on her way down?'

There was a slight pause before Joyce said uncertainly, 'Perhaps she thought she heard someone upstairs, and went to investigate.'

'Why should she? Both Grant and Belinda had every right to be up there. You don't think she had a visitor – someone she had arranged to see?' Karen suggested.

'That wouldn't explain why she was on the stairs,' Joyce said reasonably. 'In any case, Anna's never had visitors before. I don't even know if she has any friends, apart from us.'

'She's been . . . different, lately. As though she had something on her mind. As though she knew something.'

'Oh, Karen,' Joyce burst out with sudden anger, 'we've all been different lately. Don't start reading mysteries into everything, please!'

Belinda started to speak, but Grant raised his voice above hers. 'We're all under a lot of strain. I think we all deserve a rest.'

Sixteen

Without Anna in it, the roomy kitchen seemed unreal, and Karen found herself glancing round nervously as she washed up the coffee cups. She put on the radio and tried to follow the music being played, but her mind kept picturing the housekeeper's still shape on the hall floor, with red ribbons of blood trailing through her grey hair. Why had she been upstairs, or on her way back down? What, or who, could have caused her to exchange the kitchen, her usual haunt, for the upper flat when, as far as Karen knew, she had not set foot there since the day Karen herself had moved back downstairs, her marriage over?

She jumped as the phone on the kitchen wall rang, and ran to pick it up. It was Charlie. 'I've just heard; how's Anna?'

'Unconscious, and they think she'll stay like that for . . .' Karen stopped and swallowed hard, then said carefully, '. . . for hours, perhaps days. They'll let us know as soon as there's any change.'

'I can't believe it! Accidents just don't happen to people like Anna. They don't dare to happen.'

'That's what I thought too.'

'Is there anything we can do? Would you like me to come round?'

'There's no need, really.' Karen assured her friend that she would be informed as soon as there was any change, then hung up as Joyce came in.

'Who was it?'

'Charlie Leslie.'

'Oh. I thought it might be the hospital.'

140

'From what they said earlier, I doubt if we'll hear anything tonight.'

Joyce nodded, pushing back a lock of hair that had fallen over her forehead, then said, 'You don't mind if I lie down for a while, do you, dear?'

'Of course not.'

'You should do the same. You look worn out.'

'I will,' Karen said, but when her aunt had gone she sat down at the kitchen table, running the same film – the sprawled figure, the blood in Anna's hair – over and over again in her mind.

'Look,' Belinda said, 'the woman is old and shaky. She lost her footing and fell, and that's an end to it!'

'But why was she on the stairs to begin with?'

'How should I know? Perhaps she creeps up here when we're both out to have a good nose around.'

'Anna would never do that.'

'Anna would never do that,' Belinda mimicked her brother. 'You and Karen just can't see past her, can you? You're so alike!'

'Perhaps that's why we couldn't live together.'

'As far as that's concerned, the fault's all Karen's.'

'It takes two . . .'

'Not when one of them is Karen Fletcher.' Belinda's lower lip began to protrude in a way that her brother knew well. 'I can't think what you all see in her. You, Leigh . . .'

'Belinda, jealousy doesn't suit adults,' Grant said patiently. 'I think it's time that you accepted that Leigh is more interested in Karen than he is in you. Why don't you look elsewhere for a partner?'

He had meant it as a piece of sound advice, but as the colour rose in his sister's face and her green eyes narrowed to become shards of glittering glass he realised that he had made a mistake.

'Perhaps you should take a good long look at yourself instead of criticising me,' Belinda hissed, 'and then perhaps you would stop fawning round Karen. She's not going to take you back, you know. Now that she owns Fletcher's and she's got Leigh back on a lead, she doesn't need you any more.'

'I know that my marriage is well and truly over, Belinda.'

'Really? It's hard to tell. You defend Karen every chance you get. It's pathetic!'

'I defend her because you never miss a chance to sneer at her. You've disliked her from the beginning and you've never made the slightest attempt to conceal it, although you were happy enough to take advantage of her generosity.'

'I only moved into this flat to keep you company! I would have much preferred to live somewhere else.'

'Don't be so sanctimonious; you moved in because you needed somewhere to stay after your own marriage broke down and you came back from Canada. You wanted to be fussed over and sympathised with, and you were; but now I'm tired of propping you up, Belinda. We're both adults and we both have our problems – who hasn't? And one of your main problems is that you've been spoiled all your life.'

'How dare you speak to me like that? If Mother and Father could hear you now . . .'

'I wish they could. I wish they were here to see for themselves what they turned you into, Belinda. Oh, I know that I'm to blame as well, and so is that poor husband of yours. There's always been something about you that makes people want to protect you. The problem is that you use it to your own advantage. At times like this', Grant said, surprised by his own honesty, 'I can fully understand why your marriage ended.'

'At least I walked away from it,' she blazed at him. 'I didn't hang around the way you hang around Karen, currying favour.'

'I work at Fletcher's, so of course I have to stay in the area. And as for me staying on in this flat, that arrangement suited us both.'

'Of course it did – it suited her to have you near to hand if she ever needed you for anything, and it gave you the opportunity to hang around her heels like that wretched little dog of hers.'

'I think you've said enough, Belinda,' Grant told her coldly. 'Stop now, or . . .'

'Or what?' She widened her eyes dramatically. 'You don't mean that I might be the next victim in this weird crime explosion that only exists in Karen's fevered brain? Oooohhh!'

Grant took a step forward, then halted, his hands clenching by his sides. 'If there is a murderer in the area,' he said coldly, quietly, 'then I certainly think that that vicious tongue of yours could make you his next victim.'

Belinda opened her mouth to speak and then shut it again, eyeing him warily. Then she turned and flounced away. At the door of her room she paused.

'I'm going away tomorrow for several days, to visit a friend.'

'I didn't know you had any friends.'

'I have plenty! And while I'm there, I'll look for a new job, and somewhere to live. This place bores me to tears.'

Then the door slammed hard behind her, and Grant let out his breath in a long sigh, forcing his fists to relax and open out.

Supper was a sketchy affair that night, prepared by Joyce and Karen because they felt an unspoken need to keep some sort of routine in their shattered lives. The phone shrilled from time to time, and they took turns to answer it. Almost every call was from someone enquiring after Anna. Karen had never realised before how many people cared for the old woman.

'They all mean well, but I wish we could take the phone off the hook and get some peace,' she said as she hung up after yet another call. 'But I keep thinking that every call is from the hospital.' She rubbed her eyes and yawned. 'I think we should both have an early night. I can take calls on the phone in my room.'

Joyce insisted on giving her one of the sleeping pills that she used regularly, but instead of swallowing it, Karen left it on her dressing table. The hospital might call, and she didn't want to miss a summons. An hour after putting the light out, still tossing and turning, she suddenly remembered what Anna had

143

said to her about loyalty, and things going on for long enough. She struggled to recall the words, and although they danced tantalisingly around, her mind was too tired to catch them.

She turned over, trying to find a more comfortable position, then froze as a sudden gleam of light caught her attention. The door handle was turning slowly, so slowly that only the sudden tiny flash of light round its rim betrayed the movement.

The terror of that night when she had been attacked in her sleep rushed back. Even though she knew that she had locked the door, Karen felt giddy with fear as she watched the knob's slow, silent progress.

With trembling fingers she snatched at the bedside telephone, almost knocking it off the table. As she stabbed at the number the handle stopped moving, then knuckles rapped softly at the door.

'Karen? Are you awake, dear? I thought you might like a cup of tea.'

Karen put the phone down, choking back hysterical laughter as she slid out of bed and went to open the door. Joyce stood outside, a tray holding a teapot and two cups in her hands.

'Did I waken you, dear?'

'No, but you gave me the fright of my life.'

'Oh, Karen, I am sorry. I meant to glance in to see if you were asleep, but the door was locked?' She followed Karen into the room then said, after one look at the tumbled bed, 'You've not had any sleep at all, have you? Nor could I. That's why I got up and made the tea. Now then . . .'

Karen could have done without the tea, but she knew that preparing and sharing it was helping her aunt, so she accepted her cup with thanks and resigned herself to the company.

'Darling, I'm sorry I jumped down your throat earlier, in front of everyone,' Joyce burst out after a brief silence. 'I don't know what came over me!'

'It's all right, Joyce; we're all behaving rather badly just now. Why don't you bring your tea over here?' Karen suggested, drawing back the bedclothes; 'then we can cuddle up the way we used to do when I was little and couldn't sleep.'

Joyce accepted with enthusiasm. 'Just like the old days,' she said when they were both curled up in Karen's bed, the tray balanced on their knees. 'It was nice when you used to come into my bed for a cuddle. It made me feel wanted.'

'You always were.'

'If Dan was home, you always went to him instead,' Joyce said wistfully. 'You only came to me when he was out.'

'Oh, Joyce!' Impulsively, Karen hugged the other woman. 'You were always so good to me, and I took you for granted. You and Anna were like mothers to me.'

'I never saw myself as a mother,' Joyce said, and drained her cup. 'But I wish I had. Things could have been so much better.'

In the morning, Anna's condition was unchanged. Karen sat by her bed for a while, willing her to open her eyes and to speak. She was convinced that all the pieces lay locked in that broken, bandaged head; but Anna's stubby lashes remained motionless on her pale, sunken cheeks, and her bloodless mouth stayed silent.

'She could waken at any time,' the nurse volunteered gently.

'Or she could stay like this for months.'

'We have to hope for the best.'

Taking one last look before she rose to go, Karen wondered bleakly if Anna would ever again open her eyes, or tell anyone what had happened to her.

Sam Crombie had arrived at the house first thing that morning, catching her just as she was about to leave for the hospital. She had told him about Anna's cryptic words on the night the wheel had come off Leigh's car.

'Loyalty can only go so far. The time's come for things to be said,' he repeated slowly. Are you sure of that, Mrs Roberts?'

Karen nodded. 'And she said something about other people needing to get themselves sorted out. I think that Anna knew who was behind all the things that have been happening, and she was going to face them with it.'

'And then whoever it was pushed her down the stairs?'

'I can't accept that she tripped and fell. In any case, what was she doing there in the first place?'

'Perhaps she went to speak to Mr Roberts or his sister.'

'They weren't in the flat at that time. She could have heard something, or seen someone who shouldn't have been there,' Karen suggested. Then, as he said nothing, she blundered on, 'We won't know the truth until Anna tells us. And if I'm right, Anna could be in danger.'

'I doubt that, Mrs Roberts. But I'll go along to the hospital later, have a word with them.'

At least, Karen thought as she left the busy ward, Anna was surrounded by other patients. If someone did bear her ill will, they would find it difficult to harm her with so many people around.

Seventeen

Karen drove beneath the big archway made up of the phrase 'Fletcher & Co.,' in large letters, and managed to park her car near the door. Locking the car, she turned and looked back at the gate, catching her lower lip between her teeth. Then she turned her back on it, and headed towards Leigh's office, meeting Grant on his way out.

'It's not bad news, is it?' he asked immediately. 'I telephoned the hospital just a few minutes ago; they said that there was no change.'

'I know, I've just come from there.'

'Three days . . . you would have thought that she would have come round by now.'

'Apparently it's not unusual.'

'It is when you've never experienced something like this before. Are you looking for me?'

'Leigh's taking me to lunch.'

'Ah.' He hesitated, then said, 'I owe you an apology over Belinda's behaviour that night.'

'Surely that's up to Belinda herself.'

'She gone off to stay with a friend and I don't expect her back.'

'Oh.' She could think of nothing else to say.

'Are you going back to the hospital this afternoon?'

Karen nodded. 'Joyce has promised to do some shopping for Mrs Blair, so I'll go to the hospital this afternoon and she'll go in the evening. I sat with Anna this morning, willing her to wake up and give me a row for something – anything. She's so still, Grant. Like a wax model of herself . . .' Her voice began to wobble and he put a hand on her arm.

'She'll come round soon,' he said, more in hope than certainty.

'You really think so?'

'Of course. Anna wouldn't let a little accident like that keep her down for long.'

Her step, as she went on to Leigh's office, had more of a spring in it than before. It was a relief to know that, for the time being at least, she was free of Belinda's sulks and her spiteful comments.

'What you need,' Leigh said, as he started the car ten minutes later, 'is a holiday. An exotic beach somewhere, and a comfortable hotel, and you and me far from all our worries and cares.'

'It sounds wonderful, but I can't leave Anna.'

'I was talking about later on, when she's fully recovered . . . and she will recover,' he reassured her, reaching out to put a hand over hers. 'I could book it now, for two weeks ahead.'

'It sounds lovely,' she admitted, cheered by his assumption that within two weeks Anna would be well.

'I'll go ahead and book, then. Now sit back and choose your ideal holiday spot.'

'I can't think of anywhere,' Karen said, when they were settled at a corner table in the restaurant. 'Why don't you decide?'

'Fine. Somewhere warm and lazy. It will be the beginning of the rest of our lives, because I've made up my mind that things are going to change from now on.'

'In what way?'

'Well, during the holiday I want you to settle on a wedding date. I mean it, Karen,' he added quickly as she began to speak; 'I can't bear to see you so unhappy, and so alone. We need each other, darling, and I've waited long enough – you can't deny that. See your lawyer about the divorce, please, and we can marry as soon as it comes through.'

'Would it sound Victorian if I said that this is so sudden?'

A grin split his face. 'Don't let's do Victorian . . . unless you want me to go down on my knees in front of all these people and propose properly. But if you insist . . .' He threw his napkin down and began to push his chair back.

'Don't you dare!' To her surprise, a laugh bubbled to the surface. In many ways Leigh reminded her of Dan; she had a suspicion that that was why she had fallen in love with him in the first place. But the similarity had never been as strong as it was at that moment.

'I give in,' she said. 'Yes, I will marry you,' and as he reached across to cover her hand with his, she felt truly loved and protected for the first time since her father's death.

During the rest of the meal they made plans . . . crazy, carefree plans for the future they were going to share. All at once it seemed to Karen that the divorce would take an unbearably long time to come through.

'Nothing compared to the time we've already waited . . . and wasted,' Leigh said. 'Did you think we could find a way of asking Grant to move out, so that we can put your house back to the way it should be? Now that you're going to become more involved in the business, we could do with a proper office there, so that—'

'Leigh . . . I haven't had time to talk to you about this. I've decided to sell out.'

His dark-blue eyes went blank with shock. 'Sell the firm? But surely, now that we're going to be together . . .'

'I can't seem to get into the business, and I don't want to go back to the old days, just being a figurehead. I want to sell everything, Leigh – the house as well as the business – and start all over again with a new marriage and a new life.'

'But . . .' He swallowed, looking down at his hands, then up at her. 'There's such a lot I want to do there. I have so many plans, and now that we're going to be a partnership . . .'

'There are other companies. You could even start up on your

own if you want. We could afford that, with the money we'll realise from the house, and the business.'

'What about Joyce? Where will she go when you sell her home from beneath her?'

'You surely don't think that I would desert her? She'll make her home with us, wherever it is.'

'And if she doesn't want that?'

'Then we'll buy her a place of her own, wherever she wants. London, perhaps; she might want to go back there.'

Leigh ran a hand through his hair. 'It's a big decision to make, darling. You must take time to think it over.'

'That's what Grant said.'

'You told him before you told me?'

'It's just the way it happened. I made up my mind on my way home from that last meeting, when you and Grant were at loggerheads. I just couldn't bear the thought of going on like that, Leigh. Then Grant came to the house to find out why I hadn't gone to his office with the rest of you to see the new material, and I blurted it out then. He was furious.'

'I can understand that. We've all devoted ourselves to keeping Fletcher's going when others like it have fallen by the wayside.'

'And thanks to your hard work this is the right time to find a buyer willing to take over a viable business. And the right time for me – for us – to look to the future. Divorcing Grant is only the beginning; I need to make a clean sweep altogether, and that means moving away from here. The firm that made the takeover offer may still be interested,' she offered, watching as he chewed thoughtfully on his lower lip.

'They might. Do you want me to test them out?'

'Would you?' She was grateful to see that, now the first shock of hearing her decision was past, he was on her side.

'On condition that you talk to your lawyer about it tomorrow, Karen. Don't rush into anything. I want you to make sure that you know what you're doing, and that it's really what you want.'

'I'll phone him this afternoon. Leigh, you really wouldn't mind if I went ahead with a sale?'

He covered her hand with his. 'I have to admit that I would rather stay with Fletcher's, but your happiness comes first. Whatever you want, I want for you . . . oh damn,' he finished as his mobile rang.

'My secretary,' he said after a brief call. Something's come up and I'm needed at the office. Do you mind skipping the coffee? That just gives me time to drop you back at the factory to collect your car.'

'Take me back to the factory and I'll have a cup with Edith before I drive myself home.'

They left the restaurant to find that the skies were darkening and the wind had risen. Leigh stopped the car further along the road, and hurried into a shop, returning with his arms full of flowers.

'Your first engagement gift.' He dumped them on her lap and the car was filled immediately with their scent. 'I can't give you a ring until you've got that divorce, so they'll keep you going until I can find something more permanent.'

Rain spattered the windscreen as they stopped in the factory car park. Leigh leaned across and gave Karen a swift kiss.

'Give me your keys, then get indoors while I transfer the flowers to your car. It looks as though we're in for a downpour. I'll phone you later,' he added when she had handed the keys over. 'Love you.'

'I've just been trying to phone you,' Edith said when Karen walked into her office, 'to let you know that I went to see Anna during my lunch break, and she's still the same – no change.'

'I was thinking of going there now.'

'I would leave it till later, dear; they only let me spend a few minutes with her. Joyce had been in too.'

'I thought she was spending the afternoon with a friend.'

'She is, but she wanted to see Anna first. She's in quite a state about what's happened. The nurses told me that they had had to send her home because she was getting in their way and they want Anna to rest. I said that she seemed to be doing exactly that, and I was told that we can never be certain just what a person in a coma hears. I hadn't realised that.'

'Surely she must wake up soon!'

'My dear, I wish I could promise you that, but I don't know how long it could be. Nobody does, where head injuries are concerned.' Rain spattered noisily across the window and Edith got up from behind her desk to peer out. 'In any case, you'd only get soaked between the hospital and the car park and that rain's getting . . . Why is Leigh dashing through the car park with a huge armful of flowers?'

'He bought them for me, and now he's having to move them from his car to mine. Edith, can you keep a secret?' Karen said impulsively, and then laughed as the woman who had been her father's mistress for years without her even guessing about it gave her a quizzical look. 'I should have remembered that nobody can beat you when it comes to keeping secrets. Leigh and I are going to get married.'

'You're going to divorce Grant?'

'It's either a divorce or a prison sentence for bigamy. And I don't fancy going to prison. You don't sound very pleased.'

'Of course I'm pleased! Come here . . .' Edith gave her an unexpected kiss, then said, 'It's just that . . . I always thought that you and Grant would change your minds.'

'But I thought that you two were quite close these days.'

'Me and Grant? You're surely not talking about us liking each other in the romantic sense, are you?'

Suddenly, Karen began to feel like a fool. 'I just heard that you'd been seen together several times,' she said feebly.

'And so you put two and two together to make seven? Karen, apart from the fact that I'm too old for Grant, nobody else can ever take your father's place as far as I'm concerned. Grant had nobody to confide in over this new yarn he was so excited about, so he came to me. He knew', she added drily, 'how good I was at keeping my mouth shut.'

'There's something else, Edith. I've been thinking about that offer Jopling and Ferguson made for the company . . .'

'I also told you that it had been withdrawn when the board turned it down.'

'I know that, but there could well be other firms interested.'

'Oh, Karen, are you sure? Does Grant know about this?'

'Know what?' Grant asked from the doorway.

Karen took a deep breath. 'That I'm going ahead with a sale, if I can find a buyer.'

'What?' He came into the office like a whirlwind. 'I thought we'd settled all that nonsense.'

'I've made up my mind, Grant.'

'It has to go before the entire board. We can outvote you . . .'

'Karen holds just over half the shares,' Edith reminded him. 'And she also holds the chairperson's casting vote.'

'Even if I didn't, Leigh's on my side.'

'He knows about this?' Grant asked, stunned.

'I'm going to marry him once the divorce comes through.'

A mixture of expressions rushed across his face, and he gave a short bark of laughter. 'So the two of you are driving off into the sunset and leaving the rest of us to go to hell.'

'It's not like that!'

'Isn't it?' he asked, and walked out.

'Grant!' She would have followed him, but Edith put a hand on her arm.

'Leave him be; I'll speak to him later.'

'Edith, if I do find a buyer, I'll make sure that Grant's kept on here. And you and Leslie as well.'

'Don't worry about me, my dear. Your father left me well provided for and I'd not want to work for anyone else but him, or his daughter. If it comes to a sale, I shall take a very long holiday and consider my options. Who knows, I might even decide to join another company. It's an interesting thought.'

'Do you agree with Grant? Am I being selfish?'

'Time passes and things change. You have your own future

to think of, and your happiness means a lot of me. You must do as you think best. And meanwhile,' Edith added, looking out of the window again, 'I think you should get home because that rain seems to be getting worse.'

Eighteen

The car's interior was bathed in scent from the flowers on the back seat as Karen drove home. The storm was worse; even though the windscreen wipers threw a fountain of water to the side with each sweep, more drops rushed in to smear the glass, and thunder and lightning had arrived as well. She switched on her headlights and gripped the steering wheel tightly, peering at the road ahead. It was a relief when she reached the gates and was able to turn up the drive between wind-lashed bushes.

She burst into the house in a shower of raindrops, calling her aunt's name, eager to share her news. Joyce was an incurable romantic and she adored Leigh; she, at least, would be happy for them both.

But the house was silent, and a note on the telephone table read, in Joyce's untidy scrawl, 'Went to the hospital, Anna the same. Gone to see Mrs Blair, back about five. Love, Joyce.'

Karen took her raincoat from the hall cupboard, pulled the hood up over her head, and opened the door just as lightning flashed across the garden. This time, as she plunged back out into the rain to rescue the flowers, the thunder was nearer, and louder.

She went about the house, switching on lights to brighten the place up, then telephoned the lawyer's office to make an appointment for the following morning. Finally she returned to the kitchen, where she had left Leigh's flowers, and found two large vases.

She was studying the first arrangement when the phone rang, making her jump.

It was Leigh, his voice tense. 'What happened between you and Grant this afternoon?'

'He told you?'

'I haven't seen him as yet, but I've spoken to Edith. It sounds as though you had quite a row.'

Karen sighed. 'I told him that I was going to look for a buyer for the company.'

'Oh.' Leigh was silent for a moment, then said, 'I'd hoped that we could break the news to him together, and gently. He didn't take it well, then?'

'Leigh, Grant never takes anything to do with me well. He'll get over it; he'll have to.'

'Did you tell him about . . . about us?'

'It came out in conversation,' she admitted, and when he said nothing: 'He had to know some time, Leigh.'

'I know, but . . . he's been a bit . . . oh, I don't know, a bit unstable recently.'

'Unstable?'

'It's not just been this business over using a machine for the new thread behind our backs; we've all . . . Edith and Forbes and I . . . been finding Grant difficult to work with over the past month or so. And to hear at one and the same time that he's losing you and perhaps his job . . .'

'Leigh, Grant and I lost each other months ago, and if I sell out he'll probably be kept on by the new owners. He's very good at his job.'

'He isn't a team player, though. That could go against him.' There was another short silence, punctuated by another clap of thunder, almost overhead; then Leigh said, 'I think I should go and have a word with him.'

'No, leave it, please. The last thing I want today is for you two to have another quarrel.'

'We won't, darling, I promise you. I just want to reassure him, and to get an idea of his mood. I'll phone back when I've spoken to him.'

'Leigh, no, not today . . .' she began, but he had hung up. For a moment Karen held the phone, listening to the purr of a broken connection; then she put it down and went back to the kitchen to arrange the last of the flowers in the second vase. Surely, today of all days, she had a right to be happy, and yet nothing, including the weather, was on her side.

She carried one of the vases into the living room and put it by a window, then peered out, trying to see through glass lashed and blurred by rain. Lightning flashed again and she moved closer to the glass under the impression that the sudden streak of light had shown someone – Joyce? – emerging from beneath the trees at the top of the driveway. Unable to see anything, she ran to the door, opening it on a clap of thunder. The gravel sweep was empty and the driveway showed nothing but waterlogged trees and bushes.

Shivering, Karen closed the door against the storm and fetched the second vase, placing it on a stand at the bottom of the stairs. Then she retreated into the living room, where she switched on the radio for company. The violent weather outside and the phone call she had received from Leigh made it impossible for her to relax and, after pacing the room for ten minutes, she decided to start work on the evening meal. She was on her way through the hall when the telephone shrilled, making her jump.

It was Leigh again, and he sounded exhausted. 'Karen, I'm sorry, darling, but . . .'

'You and Grant have quarrelled again,' she guessed, her heart sinking. Was she never going to be free of this bickering between two people she cared for and relied on?

'I couldn't even talk to him, Karen. He hit the roof as soon as he saw me. Accused me of encouraging you to sell up to spite him. He even said that I only wanted to marry you for your money.'

'But that's ridiculous! That's not like Grant at all.'

'I know. I was completely taken aback, but the more I tried to explain, the more agitated he became. If Edith hadn't come in, I think he would have gone for me. I've never seen him so angry. Finally he walked out on both of us.'

'Where did he go?'

157

'That's what we don't know. His car's not outside. You haven't seen him, or heard from him?'

'No.'

'I wondered if he might go looking for you.'

'Why would he want to do that?'

'I don't know. I told you, he's gone out of control.'

Suddenly she was uneasy, glancing over her shoulder as the lightning and thunder flashed and roared almost simultaneously. 'Leigh . . .'

'Listen, darling, I'm coming over, now,' he interrupted. 'In the meantime, you and Joyce just sit tight. and . . .'

'Joyce isn't here; she's visiting her friend, and she'll probably stay there until the storm passes.'

'You mean you're alone in the house?' Now he was openly concerned, and his anxiety began to affect her. 'I'm going to call Inspector Crombie and ask him to meet us at the house.'

'Isn't that a bit extreme?'

'I hope so, but better safe than sorry.'

'But Leigh . . .'

'Karen, you're safe; I promise you that I'm not going to let any harm come to you. I'm on my way,' he said; then he was gone and she was left with only the dialling tone for company.

She leaned against the table, sick and bewildered. How could Grant possibly be a threat? Could he be the man who had attacked her at the cottage and tried again in her room that night? Could he have poisoned Monty, the dog he had bought as a wedding gift to her? Could he have strangled poor Helen? It seemed incredible, but at the same time she had been certain all along that her enemy was someone she trusted, someone close to her.

She jammed a hand against her mouth to stifle a scream as the enormity of the situation burst like a star shell in her brain: Grant, his love turning to an insidious, creeping hate, probably fed by his sister's cool dislike; the two of them conniving upstairs together, hating her . . . no wonder there had been times when she felt that the house was filled with menace.

The phone began to ring and she threw herself away from it, colliding with the slender stand that held the vase of flowers. The delicate container smashed against the stairs, but Karen only had eyes for the telephone. She watched it warily as though the person on the other end of the line must see her, must know that she was alone. It might be Edith, or Leigh again, or Joyce. Then again, it might be Grant, and at that moment she could not bear to hear his voice.

Again and again the instrument shrilled before falling silent. Water from the broken vase soaked into the carpet in a widening dark stain strewn with the flowers that Leigh had bought only two hours earlier to celebrate their happiness. She felt as though the blossoms belonged to another life, a life that could no longer be hers.

Then it occurred to her: if she found the telephone so frightening, what would she do if Grant came banging at the door? She ran to it, her hands shaking as she fumbled to turn the key; then sped into the kitchen, treading the fallen flowers underfoot as she went.

With the back door locked, she felt a little more secure – until she remembered the side entrance, his obvious route into the house via the flat above. Once upstairs, he only needed to come down the main staircase . . .

The door would be locked, surely . . . but perhaps not . . . The words raced through her head, faster and faster. Was she safe, or was she in danger? She had to find out, make sure that the door was secured. Then, realising that even if it was locked, Grant had a key, she sped back through the hall and up the inner staircase, her heart thumping with the need for haste.

At the top, she glanced back down the gracious sweep of steps where Anna had fallen. Had that, too, been Grant's doing? she wondered as she ran along the corridor and down the steps to the side door, expecting it to open at any minute. But there was no sound of a key in the lock or a footstep outside – only the rain battering against the door and the thunder of her own heart as she checked the lock and then shot the bolts at top and bottom, mentally blessing her father's obsession with security.

Although their quiet, small town had no crime more serious than the usual petty incidents, Dan Fletcher had insisted on good solid locks and bolts on all the doors in his house, and in his factory too. 'What's mine's mine, and I'll not have any crooks or layabouts trying to take it from me,' he had said, time and time again.

As Karen gained the top of the side stairs and bolted the upper door, she recalled the words and recalled, too, the revolver Dan had kept in the false bottom of a drawer in his bedside cabinet. Joyce hated knowing that there was a gun in the house, and it made Karen uneasy too; but although they had talked of handing it in at the local police station after his death, they had never got around to doing it, even when the possession of firearms had become illegal.

At this moment, hurrying into the room that was now Grant's, Karen blessed the negligence that had kept the weapon on the premises. The old cabinet had been pushed into a corner, and she and Grant had not bothered to empty it out; she jerked the small drawer out with a harsh sound that seemed to echo through the house, emptied its few contents on to the bed and then slid back one half of the drawer base to reveal an empty cavity beneath.

She scrabbled round the sides of the secret compartment for several seconds, unable to believe that there was nothing there; and then, realising how useless it was, she dropped the drawer on the carpet and slumped on to the bed. The revolver had been there for as long as she could remember, and now that she was in need of it, it had vanished. She wanted to scream and kick and throw things like a thwarted child, but instead she wrapped her arms tightly about her body, rocking herself to and fro.

Grant must have taken it. He was one of the very few people who knew of the drawer's secret. Had he handed it over to the police without telling her? Or was it in his possession now, wherever he was?

She was so busy trying to think things out that she was slow to realise that she was no longer alone. There was a sense of malevolence in the air; she felt it first in her spine, then in the roots of her hair, her fingertips, her very bones. It swirled overhead then settled to cloak her as it had done before, in the living room during the party Joyce had held to celebrate her return from hospital, in her room that same night, in the shrubbery just before she had found Helen's body.

Karen stopped rocking and sat very still. She didn't want to turn round, but the sensation became so strong that eventually it compelled her to move, to stand and turn round. There was little use in denying it, for it was there and it would not be ignored.

So she turned, and she saw the gun, pointing directly at her, unwavering. She had never looked down a gun barrel before. The round, black hole was in itself evil and menacing.

She stared at it, then forced her eyes away from the gun. She lifted them higher, higher, until they were looking into other eyes, as cold and merciless as the barrel. The face, distorted by an expression she had never seen on it before, was that of a stranger – worse, it was a sick parody of a face that had once been familiar and loved.

The voice, when it came, was the ultimate horror, for it was the same as before, and that seemed an obscenity beyond anything that had happened, or could happen.

'Surprise, darling,' said Joyce.

Nineteen

'Didn't you guess, darling – not even for just a tiny minute?' Joyce giggled with childish pleasure.

Karen shook her head dumbly, unable to take her gaze from the gun in her aunt's hand.

'That's because I'm such a good actress. Dan and my parents told me that I was a failure, but I've proved them wrong,' Joyce crowed; and then, her smile vanishing: 'But Anna found out. Trust her!'

'What . . .' Karen's mouth was so dry that her voice cracked on the first word; she had to clear her throat and then try again. 'What did Anna find out?'

'That I wasn't the meek little simpleton you all thought I was,' Joyce said viciously, and Karen suddenly remembered her earlier tirade against Anna. 'Creeping around, snooping into things that don't concern her,' Joyce had said then, and she might have said more if Leigh hadn't been present.

'You said once that she was snooping . . .'

'She did snoop – she saw me hiding the tin of rat poison at the bottom of the dustbin, and she went into my room and read my private letters. But you didn't believe me when I tried to tell you. You've always preferred to side with her instead of me, your own flesh and blood! Good old Joyce' – her aunt's voice had suddenly dropped into a fair imitation of Dan's – 'quite handy to have around, and we never have to bother about hurting her feelings. Dan was always a bully – not that you ever noticed, because you were his pet, weren't you? He came to London and he tore me away from the only person who ever mattered to me, and dragged me back home

162

and turned me into the family joke. They all thought they'd won, but I had my own weapon.' The muzzle of the gun moved slightly, and Karen flinched back, imagining the impact of a bullet on her cringing flesh. 'I had patience, lots of it. I knew how to bide my time and make my plans. Then Anna got in the way!' The voice was suddenly ugly, the words coming through a twisted mouth. 'Her with her sharp eyes and her nose poking in everywhere! She needed to learn a lesson,' Joyce stated, and then, a gleeful smile creeping across her plump, pretty face: 'And she did, didn't she?'

'You pushed Anna down the stairs?'

'I came back to the house without her knowing. I came up here and made a noise. I knew she'd investigate, start snooping around. And when she did . . . she had the effrontery to lecture me! Said that she would hold her tongue about what had happened if I promised that you wouldn't be harmed. She spoke to me – me, a Fletcher – as though I was a naughty child!'

'She was trying to help us both.'

'She was interfering. You didn't hear her, Karen; she was quite offensive. I did tell you, darling, several times, that you were allowing her to be too disrespectful. You should have kept her in her place. Someone had to teach her a lesson. Well, someone did. Poor old Jill went tumbling down, didn't she?' Then, in a childish singsong, the gun swaying to the rhythm, 'But *I* got the *last* laugh!'

'How could you hurt a woman you've known all those years!'

'She asked for it! She's an old fool! A fool who thought that she was in charge. You danced to her tune, but I wouldn't. She's looked down on me ever since Dan made me come home. That's what caused all the harm: him letting everyone think that I didn't matter.'

Karen moistened her lips with the tip of her tongue. 'I wasn't even born then, Joyce. What happened wasn't my fault.'

'But you're Dan's child, and the sins of the fathers,' said Joyce coldly, 'are visited on the sons . . . or on the daughters. It was always you, you, you in this house after you were born.

Nobody gave a thought to what *I* had to leave behind. Keep your hands where I can see them, dear.'

Downstairs, the phone shrilled suddenly. The gun jumped and Karen stiffened.

'Shut up!' Joyce snapped. 'Shut up, shut up, shut up!'

Finally the phone did as it was told, and Joyce relaxed. 'Oh dear, I do hate to leave the phone unanswered,' she fretted, 'but we don't want any interruptions – not just yet.'

'If anything happens to me, Inspector Crombie will know that I wasn't lying, and he won't rest until he finds out who did it . . .'

'Of course he won't, dear,' Joyce said patiently, kindly. 'He's an efficient man and he'll find out soon enough; only it won't be me. I have an alibi, you see. I'm with Esther Blair. I put something in her coffee to make her sleep, just as I did on Sunday when I had to come back here to punish Anna for her impertinence. I'll be sitting there when Esther wakens up, in the same chair as before, reading the paper and waiting for her finish her nap. Good old, kind old Joyce.'

Sweat beaded Karen's forehead. All she could think of was to keep her aunt talking. 'After all those years . . . I can't believe that you hate me.'

'Why should I like you? I raised you because I had to. I watched my brother fawn over you and spoil you because I had to.' There was no mistaking the loathing in Joyce's voice. 'I watched you lap it all up, convinced that the whole world loved you because you were so perfect. And I played the waiting game. It's part of an actor's training: waiting, and being patient.'

'Joyce, I'm so sorry. If I had known how miserable you were, I would have found some way to make it up to you . . .'

'You never cared one way or the other about me,' her aunt said contemptuously. 'You thought more of your dog than me.'

The comment about the rat poison in the dustbin came back to Karen. 'Is that why you killed him? He was only a little dog, Joyce; what had he done to deserve that?'

'I wanted you to know what it was like to lose something precious to you, something dependent on you. Quite an effective punishment, wasn't it? That made you cry all right. But you didn't cry as much as I did when Dan made me come back home, alone.'

'And that night in my bedroom . . . ?'

'If you hadn't spoiled everything by waking up it would all have been over and done with quickly. It would all be over and done with.'

A figure appeared in the open doorway behind her. Karen blinked and then hastily concentrated her gaze on her aunt for fear that the look on her face would warn Joyce.

'I can make it up to you,' she said swiftly. 'We could start again . . .'

'Start again? How could you give me back my life, or my career, or my youth? It's too late, Karen, far too late. You have to be punished, as Dan should have been punished!' Joyce, totally oblivious to anything but her victim, gave another giggle. 'Who would believe that stupid, harmless Joyce could ever do these terrible things? Certainly not Inspector Crombie or any of the others. Once you're out of the way I'll be mistress of this house. Wouldn't that make Dan so angry? I wonder if he'll know. I hope that—'

And then she screamed, a high thin sound, as Leigh's hand shot out and clamped about her wrist.

'No, Joyce!' As she tried to whip round, Leigh pulled her tightly against him with his free arm, twisting her wrist and then kicking the revolver to one side as it clattered to the floor.

'Let me go!'

'I will, if you promise to do as I say. You hear me?' he said, and when she slumped against him, nodding, he eased his grip slightly. 'Karen, are you all right?'

'She said . . . she was going to . . . k—' Karen's jaw was trembling and her teeth chattered as though she was cold. 'L-Leigh . . . !'

'It's all right.' He released Joyce warily, and then, as she stood where she was, shoulders slumped, he stooped to pick up the gun. He opened it and gave an exclamation. 'This thing was loaded! Where did she get it?'

'It was my father's. We should have handed it in, but we all forgot about it.'

'When I think what could have happened . . .' Leigh shook his head as he extracted the bullets and put them into his pocket. 'But you're safe now, and that's all that matters. Crombie's on his way; go downstairs and watch for him – and get yourself some brandy while you're at it.'

'What about . . . ?'

'I'll keep her up here until the inspector arrives. Go on now,' he urged. Under his watchful gaze she edged to the doorway, keeping as far away from Joyce as possible. 'You'd better tell Crombie about the gun when he arrives. Given what you've just been through, he'll probably understand. Here –' he handed the gun to her, insisting when she shook her head and put her hands behind her back '– take it downstairs with you. It's quite harmless now, but it would be safer to keep it and the bullets apart.'

The weapon was cold and heavy and menacing in her hand. As she went along the corridor towards the stairs there was another lightning flash, followed after a pause by a roll of thunder. The storm was beginning to move away. Downstairs, apart from the spilled flowers in the hall, everything was surprisingly normal. She had left the radio on, and now it poured out cheerful music. Karen put the gun into the sideboard, out of sight, and scrubbed her hands against her skirt to rid them of the feel of the hard metal. Then she switched the radio off before taking Leigh's advice and pouring herself a generous glass of brandy. Her teeth chattered against the glass as she drank, and when the strong spirit hit the back of her throat it threatened, for a moment or two, to spew back out again; but she gritted her teeth and choked it down, and after a moment she began to feel its warmth spreading through her body and steadying her nerves.

As she drank, she stood by the window, watching for

Crombie's car. When a full five minutes had dragged past without any sign of it, she turned to the telephone, then checked herself. He would arrive at any minute, she told herself, and went back to the window. Another minute passed, then another, and then the telephone rang.

She pounced on it, as much to stop its nerve-racking noise as to find out who was calling. 'Hello?'

'Karen, is everything all right?' Edith asked. 'You sound strained.'

Karen let out an involuntary, hysterical yelp of laughter, and Edith went on, 'Yes, that was a stupid thing to say; of course you're strained, after that confrontation with Grant in my office. I've just had a word with him and I think he feels bad about the way he reacted. I know that, deep down, he really does care about you still, and . . .'

'Wait a minute, Edith. When did you talk to Grant?'

'Not long after you left. I gave him time to calm down . . .'

'He's at the office?'

'No, he left just after that. He may well apologise to you, and if he does, be nice to him, will you?'

'How on earth did you manage to calm him down after the confrontation he had with Leigh?'

'Confrontation? When was this?' Edith sounded puzzled.

'This afternoon, I thought.'

'I don't think so, dear. Grant said nothing to me about it.'

'But . . . Edith, I'll call you back later,' Karen said as Leigh appeared in the doorway.

'Who was that?' he asked, and then, as she stared at him, trying to make sense of what she had just heard, 'Was it Crombie?'

'No, it was Edith, asking about Anna. She thought that Grant might be on his way over. According to her,' Karen said slowly, 'he's just left the office.'

Leigh raised his eyebrows. 'And she thinks he's coming here? It's as well that Crombie's on his way.' He shrugged out of his jacket and laid it over the back of a chair, then ran his hands over his face. 'Mind if I have a brandy? It was a bit fraught, trying to calm Joyce down.'

'Help yourself. Where is Joyce?' Karen glanced nervously at the door, half-expecting her aunt to be standing there, giggling that weird, childish giggle.

'I locked her in Grant's room,' Leigh said from the sideboard. 'She's quieter now.'

'I can't believe what's happened. Leigh, she pushed Anna down the stairs, and she killed Monty, and . . .'

'I know; I heard most of what she said to you. It's hard to believe that she kept all that hatred bottled up for so long.'

'What's going to happen to her? Not prison – I couldn't bear that.'

'Probably a hospital somewhere. Thank God I got here when I did. But it was Grant I expected to find, not Joyce. Want a drink yourself?'

'I've had one. I thought the inspector would have arrived by now.'

'He must have got held up. Another wouldn't be a bad idea. You've had a hell of an afternoon.'

'No, really. I think I'll have a cigarette, though.' Karen rarely smoked, but she needed to find some way of occupying her hands, which, like her thinking processes, seemed to have gone out of control. Her head ached and, try as she might, she couldn't make any sense out of Edith's phone call.

'How did you get into the house?' she asked suddenly, taking a cigarette from an ornamental box on a table by the sofa. 'I locked everything up.'

He grinned at her over his shoulder. 'Luckily for both of us, you forgot the French windows. I tried them when I realised that none of the doors were open and there were no signs of life. More brandy?'

'One's enough.' Karen looked about vaguely. 'The storm's easing off.' She couldn't remember what she was looking for until she happened to glance down at the white cylinder between her fingers. 'Do you have your lighter?'

'In my jacket. I'll get it.'

'It's all right, I can manage.' She slipped a hand into the pocket and her fingers closed over the lighter's slim shape. As she began to draw it out it tangled in something else, something very familiar to her touch; something that, as a child, she had played with frequently.

Leigh had turned, the brandy in his hand, and was watching her. 'What is it?' he asked. 'What's the matter?'

'Look what I found.' She drew her hand free of his pocket, and uncurled her fingers. 'My father's fob watch, the one he gave to Grant when we got married. It was in your pocket.'

'Yes, that's right. I found it on my way here. It was lying under a bush just off the path in the shrubbery.'

'But Grant lost it several days ago. And Inspector Crombie said that the police had searched the area thoroughly after Helen died, looking for a . . .'

Her voice died away as she looked at the watch in her hand, with its strong, heavy chain. Then, with an effort, she went on, 'How could it have got there?'

Leigh bit his lower lip, his eyes on the silver watch and the chain coiled in the palm of her hand. 'Are you certain that he lost it, darling?'

'Yes, because he asked . . .' she began, and then the watch fell from her palm, the chain slithering after it, and thumped to the carpet at her feet. 'Inspector Crombie said that whoever murdered Helen might have used a chain.' She rubbed her hands together hard, then rubbed them on her skirt, trying to remove the feel of the thing from her skin.

'That's just what I thought.' Leigh stooped and scooped the watch up, curling his fist about it. 'I'm going to hand it over to Crombie.'

'But Grant wouldn't . . . he couldn't . . .'

'Darling, until fifteen minutes ago you felt the same about Joyce,' Leigh said gently. His free hand reached out to touch her face, but she took a second step back, too fragile at that moment to bear the touch of his hand.

'Sit down and drink this . . .' He pushed the brandy glass towards her. 'You're still in shock. I'll pour myself another.'

She batted the glass away. 'I don't want it; I just need time to think. Leigh, when she phoned just now, Edith didn't seem to know anything about your quarrel with Grant. But you said on the phone that if she hadn't been there, Grant might have attacked you.'

'Are you sure she said that? Perhaps you got confused. It's understandable, with everything that's happening.'

'Of course I'm sure! Being confused is one thing; being stupid is another.' She went to the telephone. 'I'm going to call her and you can sort it out with her yours—'

'Leave it, Karen. We haven't got time, with Grant and Crombie both on their way over.'

'The inspector should have been here by now. Did you speak to him directly?'

'Yes, before I came downstairs. He's on his way, don't worry about that.'

'Before you came downstairs? Didn't you call him from your office?'

'Yes, and I left a message. Then I called him from upstairs to make sure that he had received it. He hadn't, but he said that he would come at once.'

All at once her mind began to function again, sifting and sorting, taking nuggets of information and turning them into an ugly pattern.

'Perhaps Grant didn't lose the watch. Perhaps it was stolen. It was meant to incriminate him in my death. Only it was Helen who died, not me. And you have the chain because . . .'

'Brains as well as beauty,' Leigh said softly. 'What a team we would have made if things had worked out the way I'd wanted.'

Twenty

It was all falling into place, and yet it couldn't be right. 'You killed Helen?'

'And you almost killed me when you walked into the study that night. I thought you had returned from the dead. But when I went to the shrubbery, there was poor Helen. Just her hard luck, being in the wrong place at the wrong time. At least you came running to me and not back to your house, and that gave me time to retrieve the watch chain. No point in getting Grant accused of committing the wrong murder, was there?'

'And the car accident . . . ?'

'Guilty, m'lud.'

'But you could have died, too.'

'Not much danger of that, really. I knew that the wheel was working its way off and I was ready for it. If I hadn't got stuck in that ditch when I got out; or if you'd only stayed put as I told you to, and waited for me to rescue you; and if those Good Samaritans hadn't happened along when they did . . .'

'You would have killed me?'

'The perfect opportunity,' Leigh said. 'And who would have suspected me when all the evidence showed that I could have died too?'

'But why?'

'For one thing, you might have remembered about the cottage.'

Karen forced herself to walk carefully to a chair. She sat down, one hand going up to the scar hidden by her hairline. For weeks she had lived with the suspicion of danger and, strangely enough, now that she knew it to be a reality, and

171

she was face to face with the man who intended to murder her, she felt calmer than she had been for a very long time. Her only defence now was to play for time.

'Tell me about the cottage,' she said, and he moved to the window, where he glanced out, then emptied the brandy glass and put it down on a side table.

'You brought all this mess on yourself, Karen; I want you to be clear on that. If only you'd married me as we had planned, everything would have been fine. We could have been happy together, living in this house, running the business together. But you had to fall for Grant, and that spoiled everything. Joyce persuaded me that it would be worth waiting to see what happened, and sure enough the marriage crashed.' He gave her a tight, cold-eyed smile. 'Waiting makes a man hungry and ambitious, but I would still have settled for marriage with you. Only you decided to accept Jopling and Ferguson's offer, and sell out.'

'I don't know what I decided.'

'You really can't remember? Even now?'

She laughed, to her own surprise. 'Even now. Ironic, isn't it?'

'The story of our lives, my pet. I went to the cottage in the evening to talk you out of the idea, but you were determined. Nothing I said could get through to you, so finally I gave in gracefully and went out to the car to fetch a bottle of wine I'd brought.' His face twisted; his mouth hardened. 'To drink to your future, I said. And you were arrogant enough to believe me!'

'And Monty followed you out,' Karen said slowly, and his eyes narrowed.

'So you do remember.'

'Vaguely. It's like a dream . . .'

'Oh, it was no dream, my darling. As you say, he followed me, so I shut him into the car and then, on my way back, I collected a log for the fire. I was as fair as I could be, Karen. I gave you one more chance to change your mind . . . I wanted you to change your mind, to make it all right again, but it was

172

no use. You said' – his voice shook a little – 'that it was your family's firm, not mine. That was cruel. I knew then what had to be done. You turned to face me and I—'

'No!' Karen's scream brought her back to the present and she realised that her hands were thrown up before her face, as if trying to protect herself from a blow. 'No, no, no!'

Leigh walked over to her, drew her hands down, and kissed her gently on the lips. 'Now you remember. And now you know why I couldn't risk that happening before, darling.'

She watched as he walked away from her, towards the sideboard. 'You did all that – tried to kill me, murdered Helen, let Joyce do what she did – all for Fletcher and Company?'

'Of course.' He poured a drink. 'I would have been happy to settle for you as well as the business, but not you without the business. And then today you did exactly the same thing: you agreed to marry me, then said that you were selling up. Anyone would think that you have a death wish, Karen!'

He turned and, as he crossed the room swiftly, she cringed back into the chair. But he merely held the glass out to her.

'Drink this; you really do need it,' he said, almost gently.

She took the glass, its cool smooth roundness fitting snugly into the curve of her hand. 'Why does the company mean so much to you?'

'Why did it mean so much to Dan? Why should it mean everything to you? It's family – our family. It's my birthright. I'm your cousin,' he explained as she stared at him. 'Joyce is my mother. And you and I, my darling, are kissing cousins.'

Karen could almost hear the brisk click of counters as the pieces fell into place. 'Dan . . . tore me away from the only person who ever mattered,' Joyce had raved upstairs, and 'I wanted you to know what it was like to lose something precious, something dependent on you.'

'I should have known. There were times when you reminded me of my father . . . but I thought it was a coincidence. You don't resemble the Fletchers.'

'I never met my own father – an actor, I'm told – but I believe that I inherited the good looks that captivated my

173

mother. She claims that he looked very like Sir Laurence Olivier. I was called after him, you know. Laurence, shortened to Leigh. But believe me, the Fletcher blood runs in my veins, even though I've been denied my birthright for all those years.'

'Leigh, if my father had known about you he would have . . .'

'He did know,' Leigh cut in angrily. 'He knew all along, but because I was illegitimate – I'm told that "bastard" was the term he used at the time – he refused to recognise my existence for fear that it would bring shame on his precious family. No prizes for guessing where you inherited your selfish indifference from, cousin. Mind you, he did agree to pay for foster-parents – on condition that my mother knuckled under and became his slave for the rest of her life.' He almost spat the words out. 'That was a big mistake, and one you'll pay for. But she kept in touch with me, and when I left school she made me study for a business degree so that I could work my way into Fletcher's. After that, it was easy enough to work my way up and become indispensable to my dear uncle.'

The last two words were sneered rather than spoken. 'I even managed to snare the boss's daughter – and then Grant Roberts came along and spoiled everything.'

'Where is Joyce?' Karen threw a swift glance at the door. Strangely, she was more afraid of her aunt, with her twisted, hating face, than of Leigh.

'Drink your brandy, Karen. By now, she should be back at her friend's, making two phone calls: one to Grant's mobile, using your voice and asking him to come at once because someone is trying to break into the house; the other to the police, telling them that your estranged husband is here and threatening to kill you. She's very good at mimicking you, Karen.' He ran the silver watch chain through his fingers, smiling. 'And so the stage is set. The police will arrive to find a body – yours, with the chain about your lovely throat – and then they'll have their murderer: Grant.'

He laid the watch down, picked up his jacket and slipped it

on, then took a pair of thin gloves from an inner pocket. 'You and Grant have had a couple of vicious quarrels recently; even Inspector Crombie has witnessed one.' He began to pull on one of the gloves. 'And under the terms of your father's will Joyce is your heir. That means that once you're out of the way she'll inherit, I'll run it for her, and the business will stay where it belongs, in the Fletcher family.' He picked the watch up again, glancing at its face. 'Time's running out. Be a good girl and drink up. I'm willing to make it easy for you, love; your brandy has a secret ingredient: some of the stuff that I gave Joyce to help her friend to sleep. It will make you feel much more relaxed, I promise you.'

Obediently, Karen began to raise the glass to her lips while he watched her, smiling, running the watch chain lightly through his fingers. Then she lunged forward, catapulting herself out of the chair and towards him, hurling the contents of her brandy glass into his face.

As he put his hands up to his stinging eyes the watch fell, the chain sparkling as it flew through the air. With both hands, Karen pushed him as hard as she could and, as he staggered back, she whirled towards the door; then, remembering that the front door was locked, she veered towards the French windows instead. Mercifully they opened under her frantic fingers and she burst out on to the terrace, then fled down the steps and across the lawn to the thick shrubbery, water fountaining up from the grass with each step.

A swift backward glance as she gained the shrubbery showed Leigh in pursuit. She hurled herself into the shelter of the greenery and then, realising that he would be able to hear her every movement, she threw herself under a bush, wriggling in as far as she could get, curling into a tight ball and clawing her fingers deep into the earth. Although the thunderstorm had passed over, rain still fell in a steady downpour, dripping on her from the leaves above.

She lay still, holding her breath, as she heard him crashing after her. Then the noise stopped.

'Karen?' He sounded so close, and spoke her name so softly

that for a second she thought she had been discovered, and almost jumped up. Then, catching a glimpse of his legs only a few yards away, she realised that he was standing with his back to her. Although every nerve in her body screamed at her to run for her life, she forced herself to lie still, letting her breath out slowly and evenly, listening to the rustle of the rain among the leaves and the sound of her own blood thudding through her head.

A twig cracked loudly under his foot as he moved away from her hiding place. She stayed where she was, trying to map out a plan. If he had told the truth about Joyce and the phone calls, Grant and Inspector Crombie would arrive soon. If she could reach the driveway she could intercept them. Then she realised that, in her panic to find a hiding place, she had lost her sense of direction. If she wanted to live, she would have to try to keep moving ahead of Leigh, or even behind him. But move she must: she could tell from the sound of his progress that he was quartering the small shrubbery. Eventually, he would stumble on her.

She eased herself from under the brush and ran a few quick steps to the shelter of a tree, grateful for the impulse that had led her to put on trousers that morning instead of a skirt that might have caught on the branches, hampering her and ripping off little flags to lead Leigh along her route. As she flattened herself against the trunk, she heard his voice: 'Karen? I heard you, Karen. It's only a matter of time . . . you can't hide from me for long.'

His casual tone, as matter-of-fact as though they were children playing some game, was terrifying. She slithered down to the muddy ground and wriggled like a snake towards a clump of bushes, expecting at any moment to feel his hand on her shoulder, or his fingers closing about her ankle. But she made it to safety and curled up again, wet leaves in her face and her ears, listening to him moving around, trying to guess from the sounds which direction he was in.

'Karen, you can't keep running,' he said. Grant had said that, or something very like it. He had been talking about her life, her future; but now she had little chance of a future. All at once she wanted one desperately. She wanted another chance.

A sob rose into her throat and was swallowed back hard as she heard nearby bushes rustling. She strained her eyes and through the thin screen of leaves covering her face she saw Leigh coming towards her, his face gleaming bone-white in the gloom of the late afternoon and patched by the shadowing trees. Rain-soaked hair clung to his skull, his eyes glittered deep in their sockets and his mouth was set in a tight, hard smile. She stayed still, fighting the strong temptation to shrink back further into the bushes, knowing that even the slightest movement might alert him.

He paused, looked around, and said her name once. 'Karen?' Then, in a mischievous childish singsong, '*Ka*-ren . . . I'm coming to *get* you!'

It would have been a relief to give in and stand up, to walk into his arms and let him end the fear and the misery. But part of her clung to the belief that there could still be a way out. After listening for a few seconds, his head to one side, he took a step towards her hiding place, then another and another. She tensed, her hands curling into claws, ready to spring out at him. If she could take him by surprise, she might be able to fight him off and run somewhere, anywhere . . .

Then Leigh stopped in his tracks, head to the side again. She listened along with him, and through the hiss and drip of the rain on the leaves she caught the sound of a car coming along the main road. Please, please, *please*, she prayed the Fates, concentration forcing her teeth hard into her lower lip, please let it be coming here. And then overwhelming relief flooded through her as the engine's throb slowed and changed. The car must have turned into the driveway.

Leigh muttered a curse, then spun round in a circle, heedless of the twigs cracking below his heels. 'Come on, Karen,' he urged. 'You know that I'll get to you long before anyone else. Don't be difficult, darling!'

The car-engine sound faded. She lay still, trying to work out how long it would take for whoever had arrived to try to get into the house, find the open French windows, realise that the place was empty and start looking outside. Long enough, surely, for Leigh to find and kill her and then make his escape. He would only have to cross the drive and plunge through the bushes on the other side to reach his own house and safety.

She began to cry silently, helplessly, the warm tears mingling with the cold rain on her cheeks. Help was so close – she couldn't give in now. She couldn't let him win!

He turned and left, moving quietly this time. Karen slid from her hiding place, ears straining for any sound that might indicate where he was, or whether help was on its way. Trying to watch where she put her feet, moving from tree to bush in an attempt to stay close to some form of shelter, she eased her way through the shrubbery.

Then she heard her name being called, but this time it was from a distance, and the voice belonged to Grant. Joyfully, Karen opened her mouth to scream his name, then closed it again, realising that Leigh was nearer than Grant, and he would reach her first. It was a chance she dared not take.

Her wet hair had fallen over her face. Half-blinded, she pushed it back from her eyes to discover that she had arrived in the clearing that held the little summer house. At last she knew where she was, where the drive was, where the lawn, and Grant, must be.

'Grant!' She couldn't keep silent any longer. She began to run across the clearing – just as Leigh stepped out from behind the summer house.

Twenty-One

'There you are!' Leigh advanced, his outstretched hands reaching for Karen, his mouth widening into a mirthless smile. 'You've led me a merry dance . . .'

She turned to run, screams ripping from her throat. His fingertips brushed her shoulder and then fell away as she crashed into the tearing, scratching bushes. Her foot caught on a surface root and she fell heavily, feeling branches tear at her face as she went. She landed heavily, the breath knocked out of her, but she managed to twist on to her back and saw Leigh throwing himself towards her. From where she lay he seemed to be twice his normal size, looming over her like some fairy-tale giant, reaching down towards her with massive, clawed hands. She kicked hard, and her foot caught him on the face. He yelped and reeled away, giving her just enough time to twist round again and scramble on to her feet. His hand closed about one ankle, but for once the rain and the mud that soaked and coated her were her allies, and she was able to pull free and scurry on, animal-like, on her hands and feet, with no time to stand up.

All the time she screamed – wordless sounds that poured out with scarcely a pause to catch her breath. When hands seized her and pulled her upright, she lashed out with her feet and went on screaming. She had come through so much, and she was not going to give in now.

Then she heard, through her own screaming, 'It's all right, Mrs Roberts; you're safe now,' and she opened her eyes to see Inspector Crombie. 'You're safe,' he said again. 'It's over, Mrs Roberts.'

179

'But Leigh . . . !'

'He'll not trouble you again. We have him.'

Now that she had stopped screaming, she was aware of other noises: a crashing in the bushes behind her, men's voices, shouting.

'Joyce was part of it. You have to . . .'

'We know about that. It's all in hand,' Crombie said; then: 'Perhaps you could take over, sir.'

She turned towards the sounds of a struggle and saw Grant reaching out to take her arm as the policeman released her. 'Come on, Karen; let's get out of here.' Then, as she strained to see past him, 'Don't look back,' he said, 'don't look back.'

'I can manage,' she protested ten minutes later as he stripped her wet clothes off.

'You're shaking like a leaf; you'd never manage.'

'Of course I'm shaking; I was nearly killed back there. Stop it, Grant,' she protested, trying in vain to cover her goose-pimpled skin with her hands as the outer layer of clothing was thrown aside.

'This is no time to be modest,' he told her irritably, picking up a towel. 'I know every inch of you better than you know yourself, woman. Stand still now; if you don't get warmed up soon you'll catch pneumonia.'

He rubbed her down as though she was a horse and, as he worked, the blood began to tingle beneath her skin, easing the shivering. Finally he stepped back and looked her over. 'God, you look dreadful. Anyone would think you'd been mud-wrestling.'

'I have been, and you don't look much better: you're soaking wet and covered with leaves and twigs. Look at the mess we've made of the carpet,' she said in dismay. 'I don't know what Anna will . . .' Then she stopped suddenly.

'She'll give us both hell when she gets out of hospital,' he agreed crisply; then, in a gentler voice: 'She really will, Karen. She'll be back before you know it. She's started to come round.'

'You've seen her?'

'I went to the hospital after we . . . after you told me you were selling up and marrying Leigh. Crombie came in later, and then Anna started muttering. Only a few words, but enough to let us guess that Joyce was some sort of threat to you. Then we both got phone calls from Leigh. Mine said that you were in danger; Crombie's said that I was threatening you.' He gave her a lopsided grin. 'Lucky for me that he and I were together at the time. So we headed for the house.'

'And came just in time, like the cavalry. Grant, Leigh's—'

'Wait until the inspector comes in; then you can tell us everything. In the meantime,' he went on, looking down at himself, 'I'd better go upstairs and get into some dry clothes while you have a hot shower. Can you manage, or do you need help?'

'I can manage.'

'I'll just be upstairs,' he said. 'Scream if you need me.'

In the shower, she turned the water temperature up as high as she could bear it. The cuts and scratches on her face, arms and legs began to sting fiercely, and the pain triggered off a sudden flood of tears. For a good ten minutes she scrubbed her body and shampooed her hair and wept noisy, childlike howls, safe in the knowledge that nobody could hear her.

Long after the tears had ended and the water swirling round her feet was clean she kept on scrubbing every inch of her body in an attempt to rid her skin of Leigh's touch.

Finally she emerged and dried herself, then pulled on a tracksuit and combed her wet hair before following the sound of voices. Sam Crombie sat at the kitchen table with a mug before him while Grant, in sweater and corduroys, his fair hair wet from his shower and lying sleekly against his head, leaned against the worktop, nursing another mug.

At the sight of Karen, Crombie got to his feet while Grant busied himself with the kettle. 'How are you feeling now, Mrs Roberts?'

'Slightly more human than I did the last time we met.'

181

'Sugar,' Grant said. 'Lots of sugar to combat shock. And a spot of brandy too.'

'No brandy.' She shuddered. 'I don't think I'll ever drink it again, and I hate sweet drinks.'

'Nevertheless . . .' He put a steaming mug on the table before her and used one foot to hook out a chair for himself. 'Drink it while it's hot,' he ordered. If either of the men noticed the puffiness around her eyes, they were tactful enough to ignore it.

She took a sip from the mug, then shivered suddenly. 'I can't believe that it was Joyce and Leigh.'

'Your money was on me, wasn't it?' Grant asked.

'I couldn't believe that it would be you either, but Leigh dropped little allegations here and there and I began to believe him. They were going to blame it all on you, Grant. My murder, and . . .' She shivered again, then said, 'That way they would have got both of us out of the way.'

'Perhaps we shouldn't talk about it until you feel stronger.'

'Actually,' Crombie said, 'I would appreciate hearing about what happened today, while it's fresh in your mind.'

'It will always be fresh in my mind,' Karen said bleakly.

'I think my wife's been through enough today, Inspector. Going over it all at this stage will only upset her.'

'No, Grant, I need to talk about it.'

'If you're sure . . .'

'I'm sure,' she said, and told the whole story, while both men listened without interruption, their eyes never leaving her face.

'I ran for the shrubbery; it was all I could think of,' she ended, and Grant nodded.

'I had a feeling that you might be around that old summer house, and as we came across the lawn we heard Leigh crashing about. I hope,' he added vehemently to the policeman, 'that your men had to use some force to restrain him.'

'No more than was required,' Crombie said easily. 'I can understand how you feel, Mr Roberts, but it's best to leave justice to us, and to the courts. And I believe that we'll get all the information we need from Miss Fletcher, if not from Mr Bailie himself.'

'Life's never going to be the same again,' Karen said when the policeman had gone.

'Is that so bad? You're young, and you've got the guts to rebuild your life. You can still go away, if that's what you want to do. Something should be done about those scratches,' Grant said. 'Hang on . . .'

He ferreted in a cupboard and brought out the old first-aid box. 'Sit still and hold your face up to the light,' he ordered, and began to dab cream over her injuries. She bore the stinging stoically; after what she had been through, it was nothing.

'I should keep the business on, shouldn't I?' she said as he worked.

'I think so.'

'And learn to run it the way my father did, if I can.'

'Of course you can, with help from Edith and Forbes and me.' He knelt by her chair to push up the sleeve of her tracksuit and smooth cream over the scratches criss-crossing her forearm.

'I think it took what happened today to make me realise just what I've got, and how important it is to me.'

'I know the feeling. It was seeing you in hospital that time that brought me to my senses,' he said, his touch light on her skin. 'I realised that I . . . that we, to be honest . . . had been behaving like a couple of spoiled children. I couldn't wait for you to come home again; but when you did, we just picked up where we had left off. I should have listened to what you were trying to tell us all, but I didn't, and I'll never forgive myself for that. It could have cost you your life.'

'You weren't the only one who didn't believe me.'

'But I'm not like the others!' He sat back on his heels, angry with himself. 'Once, we were closer to each other than we've ever been to anyone else. I should have known!'

'It would have helped if I had tried to explain things better instead of flying off the handle every time you doubted me.'

183

'I can understand why you were on edge, after what had happened to you, but me? I suppose I was edgy because of Leigh. Ironic, isn't it? I tried to stand back and let you find happiness elsewhere, and it almost killed you. From now on, as God is my witness, I'm going to speak out whenever I feel the need, whatever the consequences.'

'Good,' she said, unsure of where the conversation was going.

Then she felt her mouth drop open as he swept on: 'So here goes. Karen, I want us to give each other another chance.'

'Did you just think of that today? Because if so—'

He held a hand up to stop her. 'It's not just today; I've been wanting to say it ever since you were hurt, but we couldn't seem to get past that stupid bickering. Now, I reckon it's worth going for it. We've both changed, Karen, hopefully for the better. I almost lost you and that's enough to make any man sure of what he wants most in life. But if you do say yes, then it has to be for real this time – quarrels and all. No turning back; we have to commit ourselves, so you have to take time to think about it before you answer either way.'

'Belinda would be furious if she heard you.'

'That's her problem. She's gone, and I won't let her come back because it's time she grew up too.'

Karen leaned forward and kissed him, a gentle kiss to begin with; and then, as he got over his surprise, it became passionate. It felt right, like coming home after a long, tiring journey.

'Anything else that madam desires?' he asked flippantly, when they finally drew apart.

'I'd love more coffee . . . but without sugar this time.'

'Then you shall have it.'

It was time to look forward instead of back, she thought, watching him as he turned to switch on the kettle. Time to rid herself of the bad memories and concentrate on the good ones.

Grant was part of the good memories. He had been there for her when her father had died, and again today, when her own life had almost ended at the hands of a man she had trusted.

All at once she knew that, from that day on, everything was going to be all right.

'On second thoughts, make it half a cup,' she said. 'I don't have to think for long.'